THE THREAT WITHIN

MA

Before there was the Phantom Menace, there was . . .

JEDI APPRENTICE

JEDI APPRENTICE SPECIAL EDITION
#1 Deceptions

STAR WARS

JEDI APPRENTICE

The Threat Within

Jude Watson

LUCAS BOOKS

SCHOLASTIC INC.

New York Toronto London Auckland Sydney
Mexico City New Delhi Hong Kong Buenos Aires

J PB STA/S

No part of this publication may be reproduced in whole or in part, or stored in a retrieval system or transmitted in any form or by any means, electronic, mechanical, photocopying, recording, or otherwise, without written permission of the publisher. For information regarding permission, write to Scholastic Inc., Attention: Permissions Department, 555 Broadway, New York, NY 10012.

ISBN 0-439-13937-6

Cover art by Cliff Nielsen.

12 11 10 9 8 7 6 5 4 3 2 1   2 3 4 5 6 7/0

Printed in the U.S.A.
First Scholastic printing, March 2002

3 2126 00125 924 6

For Nora, Emmett, Cleo, and Elliot

May the Force always be with you

THE THREAT WITHIN

Obi-Wan Kenobi stood perfectly still. He sensed no movement in the darkened room, yet his muscles were tensed, ready for attack. The only light came from the glowing blue blade of his lightsaber. The only discernible sounds were the hum of the blade and the Jedi's almost undetectable breathing. Obi-Wan had been standing in the same position, balanced on a thin rail, for nearly an hour. Still, he waited.

Suddenly Qui-Gon's voice penetrated the silence, breaking Obi-Wan's concentration. A message from his Master over the comlink was not what Obi-Wan had expected. Momentarily distracted, he almost missed the stealth-training probe moving rapidly toward his head. *That* was what he had been waiting for.

Obi-Wan turned awkwardly on the slim rail and sliced the probe out of the air. Leaping high to another unseen rail, he knocked out two more probes. A moment later the lights in the room came on and the young Jedi deactivated his lightsaber.

Obi-Wan shook his head. The exercise was complete, but the seventeen-year-old Jedi was not pleased with his performance.

"Yes, Master," Obi-Wan replied to Qui-Gon over the comlink.

"We've been summoned by the Council. Meet me there."

"Of course," Obi-Wan replied. Hope sprang within him. Perhaps the Council had at last summoned them for a mission. Obi-Wan and Qui-Gon had spent the last two months at the Temple. It was always a relief to come home when a mission was complete, but Obi-Wan did not like to stay too long.

Being a Jedi was constant work. And somehow the dedication, energy, and patience it required seemed to intensify when Obi-Wan was at the Temple, when he wasn't working toward a mission's specific objective.

Jedi never stopped learning. But after endless training exercises, Obi-Wan could feel his focus begin to slip. He should not have been so clumsy with the training probes. He should have been prepared for anything. He was growing bored, and that was dangerous.

Outside the Council Chambers, Obi-Wan spotted his Master's large frame. Even with his back turned, Obi-Wan could sense that Qui-Gon shared none of his eager anticipation, his anxiety. As always his Master exuded calm. Qui-Gon was almost always content with training and meditation alone. Why did Obi-Wan crave action?

Qui-Gon smiled and nodded at his approaching Padawan before activating the door and entering the chamber. A half step behind, Obi-Wan followed as Qui-Gon strode to the center of the room and acknowledged the seated Masters.

Obi-Wan's pulse quickened slightly. But it was nothing like the nervousness he used to feel when summoned to appear before the Council.

Mace Windu leaned back in his chair, his arm draped across the back. "We've received a message from Vorzyd 4," he said plainly. "They report that they are being sabotaged by Vorzyd 5 and have requested mediation. The planets in the Vorzyd system have never been engaged in war of any kind. But tensions have been brewing between the fourth and fifth planets. All of the planets are interdependent and a dispute between two could trigger a chain reaction, disrupting the whole cluster. Clearly this is something we wish to avoid."

"So the situation is delicate," Obi-Wan finished Master Windu's thought and immediately regretted it. It would not do to reveal his impatience to the Council.

"Very," Mace continued, appearing to notice neither Obi-Wan's eagerness nor his interruption. "And to make matters more complicated, Vorzyd 5 denies any wrongdoing."

"Before you can bring these planets together to talk you will need to assess the matter carefully," Master Yarael Poof added. "There may be more at stake here than meets the eye."

Obi-Wan saw Qui-Gon nod slowly, and knew that their work would begin before they even left the Temple. He had heard of the Vorzyd cluster before, but only in passing. The next step was a visit to the Temple archives. Mediation required a good deal of research and background knowledge. The Jedi would have to be prepared for any possible conflict.

Jocasta Nu was ready when the Jedi arrived. She spent most of her time pulling research for Jedi missions. Although she was regularly briefed by a member of the Council as to what planets or systems might soon require Jedi assistance, her ability to access just the right information at just the right time was uncanny. She could almost always sense the moment when a brewing problem was about to boil over.

The viewscreen in the archives was playing a recorded communication from Chairman Port, the leader of Vorzyd 4, when Obi-Wan and Qui-Gon entered the room. Jocasta quickly shut it off.

"Sending you to Vorzyd 4, are they?" she asked with a chuckle. "I'm sure that will be a productive trip." Obi-Wan did not get the joke. But as Jocasta told them more about the Vorzyd 4's, he began to understand.

The small planet was best known for its amazing production and sale of goods. Alone, Vorzyd 4 produced almost all of the food and hard goods used by the five planets in its system.

"All of the inhabitants of Vorzyd 4 work," Jocasta explained. "Children begin working at the age of ten, when their school cycle wanes. Instead of attending school seven days they attend six and work one. Each year thereafter they gain another day of work until the age of seventeen, when they begin to work full-time. From then they work seven days a week." Jocasta narrowed her eyes. Obi-Wan thought he sensed disapproval. Even Jedi rested sometimes.

"At age seventy, laborers are required to retire," Jocasta continued. "Vorzydiaks fear that the elderly will not be able to keep up with the work pace. Sadly, most of the retirees die within a few weeks of being forced out of their jobs. The cause of these deaths is unknown. Most retirees are in good health until they are forced to stop working."

Obi-Wan glanced at his Master to see what he thought of this practice. Qui-Gon was in his fifties, and Obi-Wan could not imagine that anyone would think of him as anything other than productive. And Master Yoda was over eight hundred years old. It was unthinkable that he be asked to retire. His wisdom was one of the Council's most valuable assets.

The thought of someone asking these Jedi to step down made Obi-Wan smile, but Qui-Gon shot him a stern look and he quickly checked himself.

Of course, Vorzydiaks on Vorzyd 4 were unique beings with unique life cycles and cultural practices. Although they looked mostly human — their bodies were humanoid but they had a pair of long antennae and slightly larger eyes — Obi-Wan knew better than to judge them by any other beings' standards.

"What of Vorzyd 5?" Qui-Gon asked. "And the tensions between the two planets?"

"Vorzyd 5 produces less than half of its planetary needs and depends largely on trade with Vorzyd 4 for its subsistence. In the past they struggled and were often in debt to Vorzyd 4, though relations between the two have remained peaceful and friendly. Debt did not matter to the 4's because they had a constant surplus. Neither were the 5's troubled that they owed so many credits to their neighbor. But now things have changed."

"How so?" asked Obi-Wan.

"Vorzyd 5 has begun building casinos. The profit they've made has allowed them to pay off many of their interplanetary debts."

"And they are no longer beholden to Vorzyd 4," Qui-Gon said softly.

"Exactly. Vorzyd 4 claims that Vorzyd 5 now wants to be the planet in power. That they are sabotaging Vorzyd 4's production in order to appear stronger to the rest of the system, and the galaxy. Vorzyd 5, of course, claims this is nonsense. And the continued accusations are making them very angry."

Handing Qui-Gon a stack of disks, Jocasta replayed Chairman Port's message. The large man on the screen looked uncomfortable, but his plea was direct.

"I am contacting you to request mediation. We are being attacked. Vorzyd 5 is to blame. All diplomats and suspected spies have been expelled. The sabotage continues. Please contact us at once." As he talked, the ends of Chairman Port's antennae moved about like birds looking for a place to land.

"It is unusual that the chairman has contacted

us," Jocasta said once the image had disappeared from the screen. "In the past Vorzydiaks have had little contact with the galaxy outside their cluster. They were even reluctant to have representation in the Senate. The fact that they have requested outside help can only mean that they feel their situation is desperate."

Qui-Gon and Obi-Wan thanked the archivist and left with stacks of additional information to review on their own. Obi-Wan did not relish the task. This mission, he realized, would not provide the action he craved. The Vorzyd system sounded dull, and diplomacy was often a long and tedious process. Obi-Wan sighed and inwardly scolded himself. He knew he should be grateful for any mission. At least it was a change.

CHAPTER 2

Qui-Gon started down the shuttle ramp before it touched the floor of the hangar on Vorzyd 4. He had spent the entire journey reviewing information about the planets and their history, and was anxious to move around and get some fresh air. All of the disks held data about the planets' corporate history, and while Vorzyd 4's success as a peaceful corporation was admirable, it had been dry research. Qui-Gon had been totally unable to get any sense of what Vorzydiaks were like as individuals.

The hangar they'd landed in was uncluttered. Aside from the workers loading cargo on what appeared to be export ships, there were not many beings about.

"Are we being met?" Obi-Wan asked. He stifled a yawn as he joined Qui-Gon outside the shuttle. Qui-Gon guessed his Padawan's research had not been any more entertaining than his own.

Before Qui-Gon could reply in the affirmative, a young Vorzydiak appeared before them. He stood for a moment, then bowed slightly to the Jedi. His demeanor was calm, but his antennae twitched nervously. Qui-Gon knew that it was unlikely the Vorzydiak had encountered beings from outside his planetary system before.

"Welcome. Follow me," their guide said without expression. He turned and walked quickly out of the hangar. The Jedi had to follow at a rapid pace to keep up.

Qui-Gon had been looking forward to talking with the young Vorzydiak. He'd hoped it would help him to understand the species better. But after the brief greeting, the Vorzydiak offered nothing more. He simply led them briskly through the streets.

When Qui-Gon tried to ask one or two questions it was obvious by the confused looks and twitching antennae that they made the guide uncomfortable. Perhaps Chairman Port had asked their guide not to say anything. Qui-Gon decided to give himself over to the observation of his surroundings. He would come to know the Vorzydiaks soon enough.

The streets of Vorzyd 4 were nearly empty. Though it was midday there were no beings about. Nor did Qui-Gon see any refreshment vendors or public spaces.

The buildings were tall and six-sided. There were no arched doorways or awnings. No large windows or ornamentation. Not one scrap of material was wasted on style or aesthetics. Everything appeared to be designed for maximum efficiency, including the hexagonal system the buildings were laid out in and their drab color-coding.

Glancing at the Vorzydiak in front of them, Qui-Gon realized that the same was true of clothing on Vorzyd 4. So far everyone he had seen wore a plain, closely fitted one-color jumpsuit. They did not even have collars.

The three had not been walking long when the Vorzydiak stopped in front of a nondescript, pale brown building. The plate next to the entrance read MULTYCORP. The guide activated the door and motioned the Jedi inside. Expecting to enter some sort of portico or hallway, Qui-Gon was surprised to find that they were inside a turbolift that was rising to the twenty-fourth floor. A droidlike voice called the names of each floor as they whizzed past. "Assembly seven, Assembly eight, Manufacture nine, Manufacture ten . . ." until they reached "Accounting twenty-four."

The door slid open and a tall Vorzydiak

rushed into the lift without waiting for the others to get off. He nearly ran into Obi-Wan.

"Unproductive entrance," the Vorzydiak guide murmured.

The tall Vorzydiak glared at the group but said nothing. Qui-Gon wondered who he was.

"Do you know him?" he asked the guide.

The guide shook his head and led the Jedi out of the turbolift and through a maze of beige workspaces. Hundreds of jumpsuit-clad Vorzydiaks sat close together, speaking into headsets and inputting information onto datascreens.

Though many of the beings spoke at once, the overall effect was a low drone. No single voice could be heard above another. There was no idle chatter among the laborers. And aside from the Vorzyd numeric symbol posted above each station, there was no way of telling the workspaces apart.

Could this be where Chairman Port rules his planet? Qui-Gon wondered. *From a Vorzyd plant?* Qui-Gon glanced at his Padawan and Obi-Wan raised his eyebrows slightly. Obviously he was as surprised and perplexed as his Master.

"Wait here," the guide instructed. He motioned the Jedi into a small room dominated by a large table surrounded by benches. Then he scurried away, disappearing into the maze.

A moment later Chairman Port appeared in the doorway. Had he not seen the chairman's image in the Temple archives, Qui-Gon would not have been able to guess that this man was a planetary leader. He wore the same pale jumpsuit as the rest of the planet's inhabitants, and his manner was no more self-assured. Though his expression did not change, his antennae twitched when he spoke.

"We are glad you have come," he said. He crossed the room quickly and sat down at one of the benches surrounding the large table. "All known Vorzydiaks from Vorzyd 5 have been cast off our planet. Still there are attacks. They want to lower our productivity. The attacks must stop."

Qui-Gon drew a deep breath. "I understand that so far no one has been hurt in the attacks."

"That is true." Port's antennae twitched faster.

"The saboteurs have concentrated on things that slow productivity?" Obi-Wan prompted, hoping the chairman would fill in the details.

"Yes. Productivity is hurt. We are unable to work." Chairman Port's head bobbed up and down in a nod.

"Why do you suspect Vorzyd 5?" Qui-Gon asked. "Have they taken credit for any of the attacks? Have they outlined terms or made any demands?"

Qui-Gon understood that after having been at the mercy of Vorzyd 4 for some time, Vorzyd 5 might harbor resentment. But taking action against a neighboring planet seemed rash, especially if Vorzyd 5 was prospering in its own right.

"We must stop Vorzyd 5," Chairman Port said, not acknowledging Qui-Gon's inquiries. "You will contact them?"

Qui-Gon was about to reply when the chairman stood. He was obviously anxious for the meeting to be over. "To work then?" he said.

Qui-Gon remained seated. He had many more questions and a strong feeling that all was not as it seemed. "Before we contact Vorzyd 5, I would like to inspect the sabotage sites. One should never be hasty in making accusations."

Chairman Port seemed to hover over Qui-Gon, but he didn't say anything.

Qui-Gon continued. "I would also like to spend at least one night here on Vorzyd 4, to get an idea of how you live . . . when you're not working."

Chairman Port's antennae moved so furiously they looked as if they would tie themselves in knots. "Not working?" he asked, puzzled. "We eat. We sleep. Nothing more."

The chairman was clearly frustrated with the Jedi's thought process. He wanted immediate action. "I will take you to the homespace when the workday is —"

Chairman Port was cut off when a laborer rushed into the room. "Vorzyd 5!" she said. "Another attack!" Her high-pitched voice revealed her distress. "Productivity status monitors are registering erroneous data."

Port rushed from the room and glanced at the nearest datascreen. "Six days behind schedule on hard goods distribution," he mumbled. "It cannot be."

Everywhere laborers stood up from their stations and looked around, bewildered. Qui-Gon noticed that when their eyes rested on the Jedi in their flowing brown robes, their already vibrating antennae would wave even more wildly. In this environment even the subdued Jedi dress made them stick out like pulsating beacons.

Qui-Gon and Obi-Wan followed Chairman Port to the turbolift. As they made their way through the maze, Qui-Gon noted a few of the laborers rocking back and forth. Others appeared to be physically ill, grasping their stomachs and leaning on their desks.

As the turbolift doors closed, Qui-Gon heaved a deep sigh. Obviously the Vorzyd 4's were unable to handle anything outside of their normal work routine. Only the chairman seemed to maintain relative calm, though he didn't look particularly well, either.

This was going to be a very interesting mission.

CHAPTER 3

Obi-Wan sat in front of the mainframe computer. He had been there for almost an hour. The Vorzydiak technician assigned to the station paced behind him, stopping regularly to peer over Obi-Wan's shoulder. Occasionally the tech's antennae grazed the back of Obi-Wan's head and neck and he could be heard mumbling something about Vorzyd 5.

Obi-Wan's Master had gone with Chairman Port to try to calm the laborers. The threat to the Vorzydiaks' physical and mental health was equal to their technical difficulties. If the chairman could not get the laborers to calm down, he would have a health crisis on his hands. Judging from the stress level Obi-Wan still felt in the building, he did not think Qui-Gon was having much luck.

Obi-Wan wasn't having much luck, either. The problem with the computer system was not a simple one. Obi-Wan knew he couldn't clear it up quickly, but was hoping to learn something about who had started it while he tried.

Then, as quickly as it had appeared, the anomaly was gone. All of the computers in the building were back on-line, running as if the bug had never been there. And there was no trace of what had happened on any of the machines.

Obi-Wan motioned to the nervous tech, who nodded and spoke into a comlink on the wall. "Back on-line. Laborers to resume work immediately."

A few of the techs nearby looked at Obi-Wan gratefully as they settled back into their workstations. They thought *he* had fixed the problem.

The rest of the Vorzydiaks busied themselves, relieved to have things functioning normally once more. Even the very sick Vorzydiaks struggled to their data stations.

Obi-Wan stayed where he was. He wanted to continue to search the systems, to see if he could determine what had caused the mysterious problem and maybe come to understand the Vorzydiaks. But the tech standing beside him clearly wanted Obi-Wan to move out of his spot.

"To work, then?" the tech asked, agitated.

Obi-Wan stood with a sigh. His curiosity was not reason enough to cause the Vorzydiak discomfort.

On his way back to the twenty-fourth floor, Obi-Wan considered what he knew. Unfortunately, it wasn't much. The saboteur had been someone who knew the computer system as well as or better than the techs who ran it. But there was definitely no evidence that the Vorzyd 5's had planted the bug. Obi-Wan suspected that the culprit was an insider — or at least a spy.

Before Obi-Wan could share his suspicions with Qui-Gon and the chairman, a long, dull tone sounded in the building. The Vorzydiak laborers groaned in unison, echoing the tone. It was a strange, disappointed sound that penetrated Obi-Wan's skin. Obi-Wan wasn't sure if the laborers were frustrated that their workday had been cut short due to the interruption, or if the sad sound was one they made every day when it was time to leave.

Like the other laborers, Chairman Port seemed to struggle to tear himself away. At last he stood and motioned for the Jedi to follow him.

Vorzydiaks poured en masse from buildings like slow-moving liquid. Though they stood very close to one another, they gave Qui-Gon and

Obi-Wan a wide berth, even aboard the packed shuttles they all rode to the Vorzydiak homespace. Obi-Wan was sorry to see that his presence made the Vorzydiaks uncomfortable, but was grateful for the space just the same. It allowed him to look out the transparisteel sides of the shuttle.

As they left the city workspace, Obi-Wan waited for the landscape to change. He'd assumed that the identical buildings would fall away and reveal the natural planet landscape, or at least some parks and open spaces. But he was wrong.

On the outskirts of the city the workspace turned to homespace. But if Chairman Port had not announced that they were in Vorzydiak homespace, Obi-Wan would not have known. The homespace buildings were slightly smaller and stationed around hubs where automated shuttles and airbusses picked up and dropped off passengers. Otherwise it looked exactly like the workspace.

There were no yards. No pads for private vehicles. No Vorzydiaks relaxing outside.

In light of this, the Jedi were not surprised to see that the chairman's home, like his workstation and dress, did not differ from the rest of the population's. He lived on a single floor of one of the high-rises.

"My wife, Bryn," the chairman said, introducing them to a slight Vorzydiak wearing a blandly colored jumpsuit. "The Jedi, Qui-Gon Jinn and Obi-Wan Kenobi," Port gestured.

Bryn's antennae fidgeted as she looked the Jedi over.

"We appreciate your hospitality." Qui-Gon offered a hand. "Chairman Port has kindly invited us to share a meal in your home."

Bryn nodded again but did not take Qui-Gon's hand. Instead she turned toward the galley. After pressing a few buttons, she placed two more settings at the table that was already set for two.

"Grath will not be eating," she said.

Chairman Port nodded.

"Will he be home later?" Obi-Wan asked. He was anxious to meet the Ports' fifteen-year-old son. Vorzyd 4 seemed so . . . boring. He couldn't imagine what life must be like for the teenagers on the planet, and was hoping that they would be easier to talk to than the Vorzydiaks he'd already met.

"After mealtime. He is working," Bryn replied flatly.

While they waited for the meal to be served, Obi-Wan and Qui-Gon looked around the small residence. It was furnished and reasonably comfortable, but revealed nothing about the inhabitants. It reminded Obi-Wan of the sterile spaces travelers could rent on Coruscant. With so many different species coming through, the quarters were designed to be nothing more than clean and inoffensive.

"Is Grath away from home often in the evenings?" Qui-Gon asked when they sat down to dine. "It must be disappointing when you cannot share your last meal of the day together."

Obi-Wan knew that Qui-Gon was also looking for a sign of emotional connection in the family.

"It is an honor to work," the chairman said tersely.

His wife nodded. "May he be as productive tomorrow as he is today," she said.

Qui-Gon and Obi-Wan exchanged a look as the table fell silent.

Obi-Wan chewed a particularly tough and flavorless bite of whatever food was in his bowl. "What do you do in the evenings, to entertain yourselves?" he asked, still hoping to spark some conversation. Though he was getting the feeling that the endeavor was useless, he felt he had to try.

Bryn looked up from her food, a confused expression on her face. "We read instructuals to better our work," she replied, as if it were obvious.

Suddenly, Obi-Wan wondered if Grath chose to work late to avoid the evening meal. He found it hard to imagine that the young people on Vorzyd 4 were as work-driven as their parents. In some ways, he thought, it was similar to life at the Temple. There, children and adults were completely dedicated to learning the ways of the Force. The path of the Jedi was fascinating, of course. Far more fascinating than anything Obi-Wan had seen here. But Obi-Wan had to admit that sometimes, at the Temple, he just wanted some time off — to take a break.

Looking up from his bowl, Obi-Wan noticed Qui-Gon staring at him. He felt his face redden. More than once Qui-Gon had seemed able to read his mind, and he hoped this was not one of those times.

Obi-Wan had felt frustrated lately, yes. But he did not wish to leave the Jedi path. He had done that once — and it had turned out to be the biggest mistake of his life. Still, there were times — especially when he felt he was not progressing — that he wondered where all of this hard work was leading him.

CHAPTER 4

Chairman Port led the Jedi into a building a short distance from his house. "This is our retirement complex. My mother lived here after she retired. Now she is dead. The room is empty," he said. His voice registered no feeling.

"I'm sorry to hear of your mother's passing," Qui-Gon said gently. "Was it recent?"

"One month ago," Port replied.

Qui-Gon noticed that Chairman Port's antennae quivered slightly. "It is difficult to lose a parent."

"Laborers do not last without work," Port replied steadily. But he stopped outside the retirement complex, as if he were reluctant to go in. "Second floor. Third door on the right," he said.

Pressing a key pass with access codes into Qui-Gon's hand, he turned to go. "Tomorrow we will contact Vorzyd 5. Work must go on."

As the door slid shut behind them, Qui-Gon

heard a tapping in the corridor. Door-lined halls stretched in all directions, and to the left a figure struggled toward them using a support. He waved to attract their attention. It was an elderly Vorzydiak.

"To work," he called in a raspy voice. "Is the shuttle here? To work." Obi-Wan started toward the nearly crippled being, but Qui-Gon put a hand on his shoulder to stop him. The Vorzydiak turned and walked in the other direction, still rambling. He had not been talking to them. He was raving to no one in particular, and Qui-Gon knew there was nothing they could do to help.

Port's mother's room was as gloomy as the rest of the complex. But it held two sleep couches, and was certainly adequate for the Jedi. Obi-Wan paced the small space between the couches. Qui-Gon knew he had been waiting for a chance to speak. A year ago he would have shared his thoughts by now. But his Padawan was growing older, wiser. He was becoming a Jedi.

"Master, I do not think that Vorzyd 5 is responsible for today's . . . mishap," Obi-Wan said. "I do not know who is responsible, but we must not contact Vorzyd 5 until we have a clearer sense of what is going on."

"Of course." Qui-Gon nodded.

"I feel . . . I feel that all is not right on Vorzyd 4," Obi-Wan continued. "There's something more here, there's some sort of . . . well, secret."

Qui-Gon nodded again. He had sensed it, too, but had not realized it until Obi-Wan said it aloud. There was a secret on Vorzyd 4. They would have to proceed very carefully.

Qui-Gon lay down and breathed deeply. Beside him, Obi-Wan did the same. It had been a strange day and Qui-Gon looked forward to meditation. But even after several minutes of trying to relax, the deep calm that usually filled him did not come.

Instead his mind was filled with images of Obi-Wan. Obi-Wan as a boy in a practice duel with Jedi student Bruck Chun, letting his anger rather than his instincts direct him. Then an image of Obi-Wan when he had gone to help him on Melida/Daan, wounded, humble, and brave enough to face his mistakes — even if doing so meant never becoming a Jedi. The boy had grown so much in the last four years. More than getting stronger and taller, he was learning to trust himself, his instincts, and the Force.

Another image of Obi-Wan flashed in Qui-Gon's mind. An older Obi-Wan, ready to begin the intensive path toward the trials. Soon he would be more man than boy. He would take the leap toward becoming a Jedi Knight.

Pride and sadness flooded Qui-Gon as he pictured Jedi Master Obi-Wan Kenobi. He looked forward to the day that the two of them would work side by side as Jedi Knights, but with this thought no image came. Qui-Gon's chest tightened. He was so proud of Obi-Wan's path, of his achievements. Why couldn't he see him as a Knight? *Perhaps I do not want to see the boy grow up*, he thought.

The whir and click of the door forced the thought from Qui-Gon's mind. His eyes flew open. Immediately he saw that the room was empty. Obi-Wan was gone.

CHAPTER 5

Obi-Wan moved silently down the hall toward the exit. Unlike his Master, he had been too restless to meditate. Though he sometimes wished he had Qui-Gon's ability to calm his mind, he had learned when it was impossible and to simply accept it. There were times when it was best to put his energy to more active use.

The corridor in the retirement complex was dim and quiet, and Obi-Wan was almost through the door when a sound broke the silence. Startled, he turned on his heels. Was that laughter?

Obi-Wan quickly made his way back toward the noise. Rounding a corner, he spotted two Vorzydiaks — one young and one elderly — together in one of the retirement rooms. The elder sat on her sleep couch, while the other leaned casually against a wall.

"Grandfather was so silly," the younger Vorzydiak said.

The elder nodded. "That is what I loved about him." She smiled, and her small, thin body seemed to surge with energy as she straightened up on the sleep couch. "He was like a breath of fresh air. Of course, we are not allowed to show such silliness. Especially not now."

The young Vorzydiak nodded solemnly. "Things are going to change, Grandmother," she said. The girl glanced at a timepiece on her belt and pushed off the wall, moving toward her grandmother. "I have to go now, but I will be back soon."

The elder softly stroked her granddaughter's face with her antennae. Her eyes were full of sadness. "Promise me," she said softly. "I do not have much time."

The girl frowned and shook her head. "Do not say that, Grandmother. You might live for a long time." She wrapped her feelers around the elder's and they stood quietly together for several long moments.

In spite of the girl's words, Obi-Wan sensed that she knew her grandmother spoke the truth. The elder Vorzydiak was quite frail-looking, and it appeared as though her life systems were beginning to fade.

"To wor —" The elder stopped herself from giving the traditional Vorzyd greeting. "Goodbye, then," she said with a sad smile.

"See you soon, Grandmother," the girl replied in a near-whisper. But she waited a few more seconds before unwrapping her feelers from her grandmother's. Then she turned and quickly left the room.

Obi-Wan ducked behind a corner, not sure if the girl had seen him. He felt a little bit guilty, for the visit was clearly meant to be private. But he was glad to know that there were relationships on Vorzyd 4 that were emotional. It gave him a sense of hope.

The girl hurried down the corridor and out the door. Obi-Wan followed. Outside, the night was dark and still. There was no sound except the echo of the girl's footsteps. Most of the planet was clearly asleep.

As the girl slipped into a nearby building, another figure appeared just outside the Ports' dwelling. It was a boy. The Ports' son, Grath, Obi-Wan guessed. He felt a small surge of excitement. He had already gathered valuable information tonight and might be able to gather even more before the suns rose.

Looking around furtively, Grath made his way across the street to the shuttle platform. This surprised Obi-Wan. If almost everyone was in bed, why would the shuttles be running? It would not be an efficient use of transportation.

While Obi-Wan hid in the shadows, Grath

waited on the platform. It wasn't long before a small maintenance shuttle pulled up and came to a halt. A second later the doors opened, and Grath stepped inside.

Obi-Wan knew he wouldn't be able to ride in the shuttle without being seen. That left only one option . . .

Quickly scanning the outside of the vehicle, he spotted a durasteel overhang running along the top. It was a few meters above his head and very narrow. He wasn't sure it would bear his weight — or if he could successfully hold on to it. There was nothing for his feet to rest on, and no way of knowing how long the ride was going to be.

Obi-Wan didn't have much time to think. At that moment the doors whisked closed. He leaped off the platform and grabbed the railing. His fingers arched over the top, barely securing a grip.

This was not going to be fun.

The small shuttle gradually picked up speed and was soon roaring along. Obi-Wan tried to ignore his aching arms and fingers so he could focus on the conversation taking place inside the shuttle. It was difficult with the vehicle's noise and the wind in his ears. But one of the portals was open, and he was able to overhear occasional tidbits.

"The meeting..." "Our best one yet..." "Our parents' attention..."

As he listened, Obi-Wan felt sure that he'd discovered Vorzyd 4's secret. The kids on this planet were up to something; there was a lot more going on than the adult laborers knew. It was even possible that the kids themselves were responsible for the sabotage.

Obi-Wan was wondering what the kids' motives were — as well as what their next prank would be — when he looked off to his right. The shuttle was about to enter a narrow tunnel, and he wasn't going to fit!

CHAPTER 6

Obi-Wan squeezed himself tightly against the side of the shuttle as it zoomed into the tunnel. The hard duracrete surface grazed the back of his tunic, but didn't scrape his skin. A moment later the tunnel widened and the shuttle came to a screeching halt.

Obi-Wan nearly went flying. Using all of his resolve, he tightened his grip on the railing. His knuckles were white and the tips of his fingers throbbed with pain. But he couldn't fall and risk being discovered. After what seemed like a long time, the shuttle came to a full stop. Obi-Wan let out a deep breath and slid carefully to the ground.

The shuttle doors opened again, and Grath exited along with the driver, who Obi-Wan now saw was female. The two chatted animatedly as they disappeared down a passageway.

Obi-Wan followed several paces behind. The

passageway was dark, and he had to walk carefully because the floor was not entirely smooth.

Grath and the girl quickly made their way through a maze of hallways and up several flights of stairs. Obi-Wan noted that Vorzydiak kids walked rapidly, like the adults. For efficiency, he supposed. But their animated discussion was nothing like their parents' clipped method of communicating.

When they emerged at the top of the stairs they were in a deserted office building. Empty desks and dusty tables and chairs were scattered around the space, which had clearly not been used for a while. A small group of kids had already gathered in a large, empty office. Obi-Wan decided not to enter the room, and hid under a large desk just outside the door.

"What took you so long?" one of the kids asked as Grath and the girl entered the office.

"Shuttle hang-up," Grath replied slowly.

There was a pause, and for a moment Obi-Wan was worried that Grath was talking about him. But he couldn't imagine why Grath would pretend not to see him if he had.

"Nania was late," Grath added.

Obi-Wan breathed a sigh of relief.

"My parents were watching me like a pair of harks," Nania explained. "I had to wait until they were asleep."

"Well, you're here now," a boy's voice said. "The Freelies meeting can officially begin."

There was a moment of silence while the kids all dropped their hands to their sides. Then everyone spoke at once. The words "It is to remain secret. It is to remain peaceful. It is to remain a surprise," echoed off the walls.

Obi-Wan was struck by how different this chanting was compared to the low drone the laborers made at the end of their workday. The kids' chant sounded alive and full of energy.

With the rules recited, the meeting began in earnest. From what Obi-Wan could gather, it centered around the youth reporting on their latest pranks and acts of sabotage. They took turns speaking, telling one another what they had done and how things had turned out. There was a lot of excitement in the voices, but the teens also waited patiently to speak. The meeting was energetic but orderly.

"We changed the traffic signals and the workers were an hour late for their posts," a boy reported.

"My father came home furious about that," a girl piped up. "But I think I saw my mother smile when he told her about it."

"Good," Grath said. "We want to get them thinking."

"The fake work orders we gave at the electronics factory really got everyone confused," someone else said. "They were actually putting the machines together the wrong way for half the morning."

"I heard those machines played music instead of giving off static," reported another voice.

"Did they know it was music?" a girl asked.

As Obi-Wan listened, he felt torn. He was not sure that what the kids were doing was right. He had seen firsthand that it was causing confusion and distress to the adults. And the accusations against Vorzyd 5 were unfair. But he had to admit that if he were a boy on Vorzyd 4, he would get pleasure out of pulling pranks such as these — especially if faced with the bleak, work-filled future that lay ahead. And the kids were working together, putting their minds to creative use. Not to mention that they clearly trusted, liked, and relied on one another. That was more than many of the laborers could say.

Besides, Obi-Wan reasoned, nobody was really getting hurt. The Freelies' own rules plainly stated that the pranks were to be peaceful. And though he couldn't be certain, he suspected that they had a good motive. One Obi-Wan could believe in.

All of a sudden, images of Melida/Daan flashed in Obi-Wan's head. Death, destruction . . .

Melida/Daan was a planet ravaged by generations of civil war, and a group there called the Young was trying to bring an end to the fighting. Obi-Wan had felt strongly about the Young's cause, and had even left the Jedi path to join them.

The decision had been a mistake. While the ideas of the Young were just and good, the situation was complicated. There was fighting among the leaders, and deceit between the generations. Many of the Young were killed, and there was much bloodshed on the planet. Obi-Wan had been caught in the battle. When it was all over he felt as ravaged as the planet itself. He was grateful that the Jedi Council had agreed to take him back. He knew from experience that it was dangerous to believe too quickly in the causes of others.

Suddenly Obi-Wan felt crowded under the desk. He needed air and space. Sitting up, he felt better and could actually see the kids in the office. He noticed that some of them had adorned their jumpsuits with brightly colored scraps of fabric. Others wore homemade hats or bandannas on their heads. The group was still talking animatedly. Lost in his observations, Obi-Wan did not see the Vorzydiak girl coming toward him.

"Hey, what are you doing out here?" she asked.

Startled, Obi-Wan looked up and quickly pulled his hood over his head to hide the fact that he did not have antennae. Luckily the office building was quite dark.

"I'm not feeling well," Obi-Wan said, getting slowly to his feet. "I came out here to rest. But I think I should just go home."

The girl eyed him curiously. "What's with the funny clothes?" she asked.

Obi-Wan looked down at his Jedi robe. "It's my new bathrobe. I had to sneak out at the last minute and didn't have time to change." He looked at the girl's plain tunic and hoped that Vorzydiaks had different nightclothes. "Weird, isn't it?" he added shyly.

"I guess," the girl replied. Obi-Wan thought she looked a little doubtful, but she smiled casually before he headed down the corridor and out the door.

As he made his way down the steps, he heaved a sigh of relief. So far, so good.

CHAPTER 7

Qui-Gon opened his eyes and sat up in a single fluid movement. The room was dark, but he did not need to look at his timepiece to know that it was very late. He did not need to see the empty couch to know that the room was still empty. Obi-Wan had not returned.

Where is he? Qui-Gon thought in frustration. *He should have conferred with me before leaving.*

Reaching into his Jedi robe, he found his comlink and switched it on. He was about to contact his Padawan when something told him not to.

Let the boy do some exploring. He is not a child who needs constant instruction any longer. He may be doing something important. And his investigations may prove fruitful to the mission.

Qui-Gon put his comlink away with a sigh. Again he was bombarded with images of his Padawan — images of a talented, impatient boy becoming a man. They had been through a lot together — revenge, deceit, war, death. And things had not always been smooth between them. They each had a strong will and those wills sometimes clashed. But they had also grown to depend on and trust each other. More than a formidable Jedi team, they loved each other and were true friends.

As he looked around the empty room, Qui-Gon wanted Obi-Wan to stay a young man forever. He did not want him to change, to grow up.

If he does, I will lose him, he thought. *Just as I have lost Tahl.*

Qui-Gon was horrified at his own desire — how could he want such a thing? Obi-Wan had his own life to live, his own destiny. It was not Qui-Gon's place to interfere with or wish it to be any different than it was meant to be.

As he lay back on his sleep couch, guilt and sadness kept him awake. He tried to let the emotions flow out of him.

It was a long time before they finally did.

Qui-Gon was resting peacefully when Obi-Wan returned. As the door slid closed behind his Padawan, Qui-Gon sensed his excitement. Energy sparked from the boy like an electric current. Qui-Gon sat up.

Obi-Wan turned on a soft light and sat down

on his sleep couch. "Master," he said, his eyes shining. "I have news. I have learned many things that will help us in this mission."

Qui-Gon smiled. Just a year or so ago Obi-Wan would have burst out with whatever news he had like an excited boy. Now he was introducing it in a logical fashion, in spite of his stimulated state.

"Go on," Qui-Gon prodded gently.

"There are two things," Obi-Wan explained. "The first is that Vorzydiaks are capable of sharing strong emotional bonds. I saw a young girl with her grandmother, and it was clear from their interaction that they loved each other very much."

Qui-Gon was glad to hear this news. Somehow it was comforting to know that the Vorzyd 4's had more emotions than they usually displayed. "And the other piece of information?"

"That is even bigger news," Obi-Wan said. "Vorzyd 5 is definitely not responsible for the pranks."

Qui-Gon raised an eyebrow. "And I assume you are going to tell me who is?" he asked.

Obi-Wan inhaled slightly. "Freelies — Vorzydiak kids."

Qui-Gon was quiet for a moment, letting this information sink in. It changed their mission considerably.

"I followed some kids to a secret meeting and listened from outside the room," Obi-Wan explained. "If I can pass myself off as a Vorzydiak boy, I can pretend to join the cause and gather all kinds of information about the kids and what they are trying to do. Then we can —"

"Absolutely not," Qui-Gon interrupted. "Infiltration is not part of our assignment. We must tell Chairman Port what is happening."

Obi-Wan opened his mouth to speak, then closed it again. Qui-Gon got the feeling that it took all of his Padawan's resolve not to explode in frustration.

Obi-Wan took some time to gather his thoughts, standing up and moving across the room before turning back to face his Master. Qui-Gon could almost see his mind working.

"This society is clearly unhealthy," Obi-Wan finally said in a calm voice. "It is not working for its people. The youths' actions are an obvious cry for help. If we are not careful about how we expose their involvement, we risk ruining everything. We may as well say good-bye to any hope of change."

Obi-Wan stopped speaking for a minute but continued to look his Master in the eye. Qui-Gon sensed that he was not going to back down.

"The Vorzydiak 4's would be better served if we prepare both sides for the confrontation ahead," Obi-Wan finished. "It will still be a mediation, just not between the parties we expected."

Qui-Gon looked at his Padawan. He stood near the doorway, his arms crossed over his chest. His eyes burned with determination, but not an angry one. He simply believed that this was the best path for the mission to take.

Qui-Gon disagreed. They had not been summoned by the Council to infiltrate the Vorzydiaks. They should simply explain that Vorzyd 5 was not to blame and leave Vorzyd 4 to sort out its own troubles. The Jedi were keepers of peace, not politicians or spies.

But then, missions often didn't go as planned. And this one was no exception. Nothing on Vorzyd 4 was as they'd expected. The dinner they'd shared with the Ports was not just culturally different, but stifled and awkward. He'd sensed that Bryn was unhappy, perhaps even depressed. Relations between the generations could certainly be described as unhealthy. But was this the way to fix it, and was doing so within their mandate?

Qui-Gon stood up and paced the room. Wasn't he constantly telling Obi-Wan to trust his instincts? How could he give the boy such guidance and then never let him act on it?

Because you are afraid to let him go, afraid of the day you won't be his Master.

"Master?" Obi-Wan's voice cut into Qui-Gon's thoughts. He had not meant to be silent for so long. Obi-Wan was looking at him, waiting patiently for a response.

Qui-Gon exhaled a long breath. "You may gather information for three days," he said. "But you must keep me informed of all happenings. And if after that time you have not convinced the Freelies to come forward and discuss matters with the adults themselves, I will have to report their involvement in the pranks to Chairman Port."

Obi-Wan dropped his hands to his sides and smiled. His blue eyes clearly showed his gratitude. "Thank you," he said.

Qui-Gon nodded. He was not at all certain that he'd made the right decision.

CHAPTER 8

Obi-Wan immediately began to formulate his plans. He was a bit surprised that Qui-Gon had let him take the lead in the mission, but he was pleased as well. It was the first time Qui-Gon had given him so much responsibility.

Perhaps he is beginning to think of me as a peer and not just a pupil, Obi-Wan thought. The young Jedi had been waiting a long time for an opportunity like this, and was determined to succeed.

Lying on his sleep couch, Obi-Wan recounted what he'd overheard at the Freelies meeting. The more he could remember, the better his chances of infiltrating successfully. It seemed he had just fallen asleep when his Master was gently rousing him awake.

"Time to get up," Qui-Gon said. "The Ports will be waiting."

Obi-Wan got up and dressed quickly. But when

they arrived at the Ports' dwelling the family had already left for the day. Cold kibi and patot panak were on the table, and the Jedi dutifully sat down to eat despite the fact that the food did not look particularly appetizing.

A message on the databoard asked the Jedi to come to Chairman Port's office in the workspace as soon as they could. He wanted to contact Vorzyd 5 immediately.

"I'll have to find a way to stall him," Qui-Gon said aloud as he bit into a panak.

Obi-Wan nodded. "I'd like to visit the Vorzyd school today, Master," he said. "There's no point in waiting for another secret meeting to occur — it would waste valuable time."

"That is probably wise. But be careful, Padawan." He paused, then added, "And I suppose I do not need to tell you to keep your eyes and ears open at all times, since that's exactly what got us to where we are right now."

Obi-Wan thought for a moment that his Master was scolding him, but his eyes showed amusement as he looked across the table at his apprentice.

"No, I suppose you don't," Obi-Wan agreed.

When Qui-Gon had left the homespace, Obi-Wan found his way to Grath's clothing container and borrowed a drab, one-piece jumpsuit. Then, to conceal the fact that he didn't have antennae, he made a makeshift turban using the hood from his robe.

"It's not exactly high fashion," he told his goofy-looking reflection. But some of the kids he'd seen the night before had been wearing doctored outfits and homemade hats — attempts to make themselves stand out and look different. If he was lucky, his hat would pass for an example of self-expression and would not be suspected as a coverup.

With a last once-over in the reflector, Obi-Wan left the dwelling and made his way to the shuttle platform. It was mid-morning, and most of the laborers were already at work. The shuttle car was nearly empty.

The city was neatly organized, so it was not difficult to find the schoolspace. Obi-Wan had assumed that the educational buildings would look like all the other buildings on Vorzyd 4, and he was right. Three identical and dull-looking structures stood in a row, housing students of different ages.

As he circled the buildings, Obi-Wan peered into as many classrooms as he could. With the exception of the students' ages, they all looked the same. Glazed eyes stared at large screens placed in the front of the rooms. Adults stood by, drilling what could only be work techniques into the students' heads. The institution looked more like a work-training facility than an actual school.

But then, Obi-Wan knew from experience that there were all kinds of schools in the galaxy. He was suddenly reminded of the awful Learning-Circle on the planet Kegan. In spite of the warm day, he shivered at the memory of the "school" where he and Siri, another Padawan, had been imprisoned.

At the School for the Learning, kids were brainwashed to believe things that were not true, and difficult or ill children were locked away — for good. Vorzyd 4 was certainly not the only place where kids were discouraged from developing their own ideas. For the second time that morning Obi-Wan felt grateful that his Master was allowing him the freedom to determine the course of this mission. To try to solve a problem on his own, in his own way. He did not want to let himself or Qui-Gon down, and he felt more determined than ever to make his plan work.

Obi-Wan turned a corner and peered into a small, square portal. Inside was an austere room. Grath and a few other kids from the previous night's meeting were inside, sitting on sleep couches. The room appeared to be an infirmary, but none of the kids inside looked sick.

In fact, they were all sitting up and chatting animatedly.

Obi-Wan stepped closer to the portal, hoping to get a better look and possibly hear what the kids were saying. But just then the door slid open and an adult Vorzydiak entered the room. Right away the kids all lay back, feigning weakness and sleep. The adult looked each student over carefully, standing over Grath for a particularly long time. Then, apparently satisfied, she turned and left the room.

No sooner had the door closed than the kids sat up again and began to talk. One of them jumped to her feet, using hand gestures to emphasize her point. Obi-Wan recognized her as the girl who had spotted him outside the meeting the night before.

It looked like the kids were planning something, and Obi-Wan wanted in on it.

Moving away from the portal, Obi-Wan focused on his body temperature. Soon he began to feel warmth tingling through his limbs — he had given himself a fever. A Vorzydiak fever, he hoped.

Making his way around the side of the building, Obi-Wan found the door to the infirmary, opened it, and stepped inside.

"The button!" someone shouted.

"Quick!" yelled another voice.

"The door!"

After a moment of confusion, Obi-Wan understood. The kids wanted him to keep the door open — they obviously couldn't get out from the inside. By pressing a button, Obi-Wan was able to keep the door from closing. The four kids leaped off their sleep couches and charged out into the sun's light.

"What happened to Tray?" Grath asked, turning toward Obi-Wan.

Obi-Wan shrugged, hoping it would be enough of a response.

"Well, I'm glad *someone* came to let us out," the hand-gesture girl said. "It was getting hard to convince the medic that we were actually ill."

"Come on," Grath said, looking around. "Let's get out of here before someone sees us."

As the kids ran down a duracrete walkway away from the schoolspace, their conversation continued.

"I think we should try to get more kids out of class next time," one of the kids — a younger boy — said. "Trainer Nalo is so obsessed with his instructuals he would barely notice."

"We can't risk being discovered," a girl replied. Obi-Wan thought she was the shuttle driver from the night before, but wasn't entirely sure.

By now the group was a fair distance from the schoolspace, and they slowed to a quick Vorzydiak walk.

"This new plan is complicated enough without getting more Freelies involved in implementing it," Grath explained. "We need them to focus on *their* part of the plan — getting the rule-following kids to think differently, too."

Grath stopped and turned toward the boy. "But it's good to keep thinking ahead, Flip," he added.

Grath smiled at the boy, and Flip beamed. He obviously looked up to the Freelie leader.

Grath ran a few steps and spun around, still moving backward. "To work, then?" he called with a smile.

The group erupted into giggles and broke into a run after their leader. Obi-Wan felt a surge of energy as he hurried to catch up.

CHAPTER 9

Drab hexagonal buildings whizzed past the windows as Qui-Gon's shuttle made its way back to the city workspace. The view was uninspiring, and Qui-Gon's thoughts drifted back to Obi-Wan.

Qui-Gon had waited outside Port's dwelling and watched his Padawan board the shuttle to the schoolspace. He hadn't meant to spy on the boy, but something had held him there. As he watched Obi-Wan confidently board the shuttle, secure in his skills and his plan, Qui-Gon felt the same pang of emotion he'd felt the night before.

The feeling was new to him, and so unfamiliar that it made him uneasy. He was not sure why he was reluctant to let Obi-Wan take charge of the mission on his own. Was it because he was afraid of losing him, or because he was worried about the boy's safety?

"Production Sector seven," a voice droned.

Qui-Gon was startled to hear his stop — and grateful for the announcement. There were no other landmarks to help him find his way back to the Multycorp office he'd visited the day before. Exiting the shuttle behind several other laborers, Qui-Gon cleared his mind. He needed to focus on the mission at hand.

All around him swarms of Vorzydiaks hurried to get to their stations. Qui-Gon wondered how the Vorzydiaks maintained their enthusiasm for work. They seemed to be in a great hurry to get to work, almost a frenzy.

Thinking about how he would stall the chairman, Qui-Gon boarded the turbolift for the twenty-fourth floor. But long before he reached the chairman's office he sensed that something was wrong. It suddenly dawned on him that the Vorzydiaks leaving the shuttle were agitated about more than simply getting to work.

The turbolift doors opened on the twenty-fourth floor. As he stepped out, Qui-Gon was met by a disturbing scene — and sound.

A low insectoid drone — much more unnerving than the one he'd heard the evening before — bounced off the walls and filled the room. Laborers rocked back and forth in their chairs like confused children, mumbling to themselves.

Inside the meeting room, Chairman Port circled the large table. His antennae flailed and his eyes looked larger than normal. When Qui-Gon entered, the chairman nearly pounced on him.

"At last," he said, his voice quite a bit higher than usual. "There has been another attack. We must contact Vorzyd 5. Now!"

"In time," Qui-Gon said calmly. "First tell me what has happened."

"It is awful," the chairman said, walking faster and faster around the table. "The worst casualty yet. The central operations computer. It controls the whole grid! It is down. We are all down."

Qui-Gon thought the chairman might burst into tears — or an unintelligible droning buzz. He had to calm down the leader. Without Port's help it would be impossible to keep the rest of the Vorzydiaks from losing it.

Qui-Gon strode to the opposite side of the room and stood in the chairman's path. Port stopped circling.

"First tell me where the central operations computer is," Qui-Gon said firmly. "Then I have work for you to do."

The chairman looked up at the tall Jedi. Qui-Gon saw something shift on his face, as if he suddenly knew he had to get ahold of himself. But he wasn't sure that the chairman knew how.

"Yes, yes, yes," Chairman Port said. "We must make our way back to work. To work." His antennae seemed to slow a bit.

"The operations computer?" Qui-Gon repeated.

"In the sub-basement. Take the turbolift to level S-one."

Qui-Gon nodded. "Contact the technicians and let them know I am coming. And when you have done that you must assign tasks to the laborers. Contact the managers. Keep everyone busy until the computers are back on-line. It doesn't matter what they do. Just make sure they are safe and busy. It is your *job*." Qui-Gon emphasized this last word.

The chairman nodded. He seemed relieved to have an assignment, and Qui-Gon hoped that simple tasks would calm the other Vorzydiaks as well. But he had no time to wait and see.

Confused laborers flooded the turbolift. Several of them were rocking back and forth. Others were holding their ears. Rather than force his way through the bewildered crowd, Qui-Gon headed for the stairs and started down.

By the time he got to the twenty-third floor Qui-Gon understood why so many of the Vorzydiaks were trying to block out the noise. The computers on the twenty-third floor were emitting high-pitched whines as they turned themselves on and off. He imagined that the sound was much worse for the Vorzydiaks, who had sensitive ears. To him the sound was irritating and chaotic. But he listened carefully long enough to realize that it was not random.

The chaos grew worse the farther Qui-Gon descended. On Assembly eight the machines on the line were also turning on and off and emitting high-pitched tones. The laborers were completely unable to cope. They stood against the walls, twitching, while gooey food product oozed onto the conveyor and then the floor.

Receiving four was no better. Huge vats that needed to be positioned under the receiving pipes had stalled. Grain was spilling out, making small mountains all over the wing, as well as a slippery hazard for the baffled Vorzydiaks. Several fallen laborers flailed on the floor while others watched in horror, too confused to offer help.

Qui-Gon shook his head. The Vorzydiaks' helplessness when things did not go as planned was extreme. He could not remember when he had last seen such rigid thinking. In the life of a Jedi, things seldom went according to plan. Thinking on your feet was a Jedi necessity.

At last Qui-Gon reached the sub-basement. There were fewer Vorzydiaks on this floor, so Qui-Gon could make out more clearly the intonations of the machines — the tones and rhythms. Stopping for a moment to listen, Qui-Gon almost laughed out loud. He stopped himself when he heard a cry. For the Vorzydiaks this was no laughing matter.

Qui-Gon ran down the duracrete passage to find a female Vorzydiak standing in a large room filled with circuits. Some of them were shorting out, and the poor worker gazed at them in horror, her arms moving jerkily up and down. She clearly did not know what to do.

Qui-Gon would have liked to have calmed the poor woman, but he knew he would be the most help if he could get to central operations. Turning on his heel, he made his way back down the passage.

The tech at the large terminal was madly pushing buttons, but the readout continued to flash. He jumped when he saw Qui-Gon, though it was clear he had been expecting him.

"Nothing is broken," he squealed. "There is no electrical or mechanical failure. It is not logical."

"It is not mechanical failure," Qui-Gon agreed. "But there is a logic to it. Your computer is playing music. It is conducting the machines in this building to play a specific tune."

"A what?" The tech stopped pushing buttons long enough to stare at Qui-Gon.

"Someone has been playing with your system," Qui-Gon explained. "Your computer is making music."

The tech looked disgusted. "That is just like Vorzyd 5. They like playing games. That is all they do," he snarled. "Playing prevents productivity."

Qui-Gon was silent as he helped the tech find and remove the erroneous command. Once they knew what they were looking for, it did not take long. And once the command was removed, the resonant tones in the building stopped.

There was near silence in the sub-basement when Qui-Gon heard a familiar scream. Leaving the tech, he ran down the hall. The Vorzydiak woman he'd seen earlier was still shrieking, but her arms and feelers were still. She appeared to be paralyzed with fear.

Qui-Gon had thought that the circuits were tied into the computer system. He'd assumed that when the computer problem was resolved, the circuits would stop shorting.

He had been wrong.

Looking closer, Qui-Gon saw that he was standing in front of the circuits for the entire city workspace. This was the grid Port had been talking about. The circuit on the grid that marked this office building was okay. But there had been a chain reaction, and circuits all over the workspace were blowing out in waves. The woman next to him pointed at the next hex of the grid set to go.

"This is the children's hospital," she whimpered. "It cannot lose power."

With nothing to go on but instinct, Qui-Gon raced back to the central operations computer. If he could override the network shutdown and flush the system, he might be able to stop the chain reaction. If he couldn't, this prank would result in more than chaos.

It would result in death.

CHAPTER 10

Obi-Wan jogged a few steps behind Grath and the rest of the kids. He was certain that one of the girls, Pel, was the one who had caught him in his "bathrobe" the night before. Fortunately she didn't appear to be suspicious of him now.

The other girl, Nania, had a familiar-sounding voice. She must have been driving the shuttle Obi-Wan had hitched a ride on. But so far nobody had openly recognized him.

Obi-Wan kept waiting for one of them to ask him who he was and why he was following them. But they never did. Grath's initial acceptance of him seemed to be all that was needed. Either that, or the Freelies were such a big group that they were used to not knowing one another.

It didn't matter as long as the students continued to let Obi-Wan tag along. The more time he spent with them, the easier it would be to gain their trust. And the easier it would be to eventually convince them to do the right thing.

Though he longed to know where they were going, Obi-Wan didn't want to risk blowing his cover by asking any questions. It would be better to listen. Unfortunately, nobody was saying much.

About a kilometer away from the school, the small band of Freelies turned in to a refuse facility. Flip and Nania began pulling scrap off a huge pile and tossing it aside. Obi-Wan wasn't sure what to do.

Wondering if the next prank involved garbage, he reached over to grab a piece of trash himself. Then Nania pulled a large piece of wreckage off the pile and Obi-Wan spotted something familiar underneath. It was the back of the shuttle he'd ridden last night. Apparently the Freelies kept it stashed here.

"Hop in," Flip said, gesturing to the panel door. The kids piled in. Nania took the pilot's seat and the repulsorlifts roared to life, dislodging debris from the viewscreen.

"Hold on," Nania said over her shoulder. With a lurch and a shudder the small craft broke free of the garbage pile and zoomed out of the facility.

Flip, who obviously hadn't been holding on tight enough, landed in Grath's lap.

"So what do you think they're doing in the Multycorp offices right now?" he asked, grinning at the older boy.

Grath pushed Flip off him with a laugh. "I don't know," he said slyly. "Dancing?"

Obi-Wan didn't get the joke, but he laughed along with the rest of the kids. When the laughter had faded Grath spoke again.

"But they won't be dancing tomorrow. Tomorrow they'll be walking."

Grath sounded serious, and the mood in the shuttle changed. The group was clearly ready to get to the business at hand. Whatever that business was.

There was not much light in the back of the craft, and Obi-Wan had to hang on to keep from being hurled about by Nania's erratic driving. As he braced himself for the next turn he suddenly noticed something he'd missed before. The shuttle's entire hull was lined with small, homemade explosives.

With a final gut-wrenching turn, Nania brought the maintenance shuttle to a stop inside a transport shuttle bay. Grath, Flip, Pel, and Nania grabbed armloads of the explosives and piled out of the maintenance craft. Despite his misgivings, Obi-Wan picked up several explosives and followed.

"Pel, Nania, you two cover the east wing. We'll do the west," Grath directed.

Obi-Wan watched uneasily as Grath crawled underneath one of the shuttles with the explosives. He needed to find out what they were doing and he needed to do it now. It looked like Grath and Flip were attaching the explosives to the undersides of the passenger compartments. Were they planning to blow up the crafts with passengers inside?

"So, I forget, when do we trigger these?" Obi-Wan tried to sound casual as he climbed under the shuttle next to Grath and began to fiddle with one of the devices.

Grath gave Obi-Wan a strange look. "Don't worry. Nobody will be hurt. That's one of our rules, remember? We're hiding the explosives so nobody sees them during the evening ride. Then tonight, when the shuttles are back in the bay, we'll trigger them by remote. So tomorrow, when everyone is ready to go to work, well . . . they won't have their usual transportation, will they?" A smile spread across Grath's face, but Obi-Wan was too concerned with all that could go wrong to smile back. This plan was dangerous, far more dangerous than changing numbers on a datascreen or giving computer systems false commands.

Grath noticed that Obi-Wan wasn't smiling. "Don't worry," he said again more quietly. "We really aren't going to kill anybody. We just want to wake them up."

Obi-Wan forced a smile and a nod. "To work then?" he asked.

"Not tomorrow!" Grath laughed.

CHAPTER 11

Qui-Gon took a deep breath and flipped a switch. The screen in front of him went blank, then blinked back on. Down the hall the shrieking finally stopped. The break had been successful. The circuits stopped shorting, and the children's hospital was safe. But it had been close — too close.

Qui-Gon sighed. He knew the next thing he had to do was to tell Chairman Port about the near disaster, a prospect he did not relish. Perhaps he had been wrong to give Obi-Wan three days. After this latest Freelie prank it was going to be harder than ever to stall the nervous Vorzydiak.

Maybe even impossible, he thought as he made his way back up to the twenty-fourth floor. He was not prepared for what he saw when he walked into the meeting room.

Chairman Port stood before a large projection

of a regal-looking Vorzydiak wearing a turban. It was Felana, the leader of Vorzyd 5.

"What is the meaning of this?" Felana demanded. "You dare to accuse Vorzyd 5 of sabotage after you have already insulted us by banishing our ambassadors? I do not understand you, Chairman Port."

"Here is the J-J-Jedi," Chairman Port stammered. He motioned Qui-Gon to join him in front of the holoprojector. "He knows the truth. He will tell you."

Felana looked even more aghast. "You have called in outside counsel? Do you think this will make your baseless accusations stronger?"

For a moment Qui-Gon was not sure what to do. This was certainly not the way mediation was supposed to work. Chairman Port had put him in an awkward position, and now it would be impossible to establish himself as a neutral party. All he could do, he realized, was try to keep the damage to a minimum.

"Tell her," Chairman Port screeched at the Jedi. "Tell her what she has done to our planet!"

"That is enough!" Felana seethed. "We have been under your thumb for a long time, Chairman. And now you accuse us wrongly. We will not tolerate your accusations."

Qui-Gon put a hand on Chairman Port's shoulder. Using the Force, he calmed the distraught Vorzydiak enough to prevent him from saying anything else he would regret. Then he turned to the image of Felana.

"Please accept the chairman's apologies," Qui-Gon bowed. "Vorzyd 4 has been experiencing some terrorist activity and he meant only to alert you to that fact so that you may be on the lookout for similar activity on your planet."

Qui-Gon could tell by the look on her face that Felana did not believe him. But she was not going to contradict him, either.

"Please tell the chairman that I appreciate his concern and assure him that Vorzyd 5 is prepared to fight," Felana replied in a cool tone. "Vorzyd 5 will not be humiliated. We are not the weak planet in the system any longer. We need only the opportunity to show our strength."

Qui-Gon thanked Felana and ended the transmission. He recognized her last statement for exactly what it was: a threat.

If Vorzyd 4 persisted in accusing Vorzyd 5 of illegal activity, the likely result would be devastating.

War.

Qui-Gon paced the long hall of the retirement home while he waited for his Padawan. He realized that he could simply summon Obi-Wan on his comlink, but he did not want to destroy the young Jedi's cover or put him in danger. Besides, he needed some time to think about what he was going to say when Obi-Wan did appear.

Qui-Gon reached the end of the hall and turned on his heel. If he did not give Obi-Wan the three days he'd promised, the boy would lose confidence. But things were getting out of hand. If Qui-Gon kept silent . . .

Suddenly Qui-Gon's thoughts were interrupted by a timid woman's voice. "Excuse me," she said.

With his long strides Qui-Gon had covered the distance of the hallway nearly a dozen times without giving any notice to the one open door. Now he stopped in front of it and gazed at the elderly Vorzydiak woman who beckoned him.

"I am sorry," she said, looking nervously up at Qui-Gon's imposing figure. "You are not a laborer are you? I thought maybe you were a laborer coming to visit. The laborers seem to think life ends when the work is finished. They are too busy to visit. But I heard someone out here and I thought —"

"I would be happy to visit with you," Qui-Gon said gently. Even in his distracted state, his heart went out to this woman.

"Oh, would you? I do not get many visitors. And do not get me wrong — I do not blame them. It is the Vorzyd way."

Qui-Gon followed the woman into her small room and sat across from her on a chair. She did not ask him who he was, but continued to talk, simply enjoying the fact that there was someone there to listen.

"We live to work, you know. Nobody realizes that there is life beyond the work. Nobody knows. Sometimes I wish there was not. The life, I mean. I wish I could die like the others. But there is Tray. Tray still comes. She says things will change. That everything will be different. I want to believe her, but they are just children . . ."

The woman stopped speaking and cocked her head. Outside in the hall Qui-Gon heard boot steps. Obi-Wan.

Qui-Gon excused himself and stepped into the hall. His brief conversation with the retiree had awakened new questions in his mind. There were many things he wanted to ask the woman, but they would have to wait. At the moment he needed to talk to his Padawan.

CHAPTER 12

"The shuttles are set to blow tonight when everyone is sleeping. Grath assured me that no one will be in the shuttle bay." Obi-Wan tried to sound confident as he reported the Freelie prank to his Master. He wanted to mask the unease that he felt. Already he thought that infiltrating the Freelies was taking too long. He wished he'd been able to keep the kids from planting the explosives, but he hadn't seen a way to do it. It was too soon to reveal himself.

Qui-Gon was silent.

"They don't want to hurt anyone," Obi-Wan added.

"Someone will be hurt just the same," Qui-Gon said when he finally spoke. "People were almost hurt today."

Obi-Wan knew that his Master was right. The Freelies *were* going too far and there was more at stake than they realized. All they wanted was to show their parents that they were alive, that they needed more from them than work training. But they were going about it the wrong way.

Now Obi-Wan wondered if his plan to stop them was all wrong, too. Looking at Qui-Gon's face, he could not help but get the feeling that his Master doubted him.

"I fear the pranks have risen to a new level. The children are in over their heads. Today Chairman Port contacted the leader of Vorzyd 5. She was outraged at his accusations and is prepared to take action if they continue. There was also an attack on the central control computer. If I hadn't been there to help, it could have resulted in a power outage for the entire city. And many lost lives."

Qui-Gon spoke evenly, but Obi-Wan felt reprimanded all the same. Even though he shared his Master's doubts, he found himself railing against them.

"I have two more days," Obi-Wan said with new resolve. "I can do this." Why couldn't Qui-Gon trust him to follow through? Obi-Wan suddenly felt desperate to be allowed to continue his plan. It seemed more important than anything else.

"It's not that I don't trust you," Qui-Gon said, locking eyes with his Padawan.

It never failed to startle Obi-Wan the way Qui-Gon sensed what he was thinking.

"The situation is complicated, and impossible for any single person to control. We must proceed carefully," Qui-Gon finished.

Obi-Wan nodded. He was prepared to defend his plan further, but Qui-Gon had not cut him off as he'd suspected he would. He was being given the freedom to carry on.

Why? Obi-Wan wondered later, lying on his sleep couch. Why was Qui-Gon letting him continue when he obviously had no faith in Obi-Wan's plan? For a moment Obi-Wan thought his Master was giving him room to fail, to teach him a lesson. But that could not be. A Jedi would never risk the lives of other beings simply to prove a point. Qui-Gon hadn't given Obi-Wan the chance to fail, he had given him the chance to succeed.

Lying in the dark, Obi-Wan felt torn. He wasn't at all sure that what he was doing was right. Yet he had no choice but to move forward.

My plan will work, Obi-Wan told himself. It had to.

The lock on the door clicked and whirred. Obi-Wan was on his feet before he realized he was awake. The door opened to reveal a very rattled Chairman Port.

"The shuttles," the chairman gasped. "Vorzyd 5 is blowing up the shuttles. The morning laborers . . ." Port's antennae twitched rapidly and the Vorzydiak leaned against the portal for support. He appeared to be in shock. "Wounded," he said in a hollow voice. "Some may not live."

"The shuttles are exploding with passengers on them?" Obi-Wan asked, disbelieving. "When? Where?"

"Everywhere," the chairman whispered. "Now."

"Contact the shuttle bay. Tell them to evacuate. Tell them to stop all shuttles," Qui-Gon commanded.

Chairman Port pulled himself together enough to hurry toward the communication station near the entrance of the building.

Without a word to Qui-Gon, Obi-Wan ran toward the exit. He could hear his Master's footsteps behind him. They needed to keep as many Vorzydiaks as possible from boarding the shuttles.

Outside, a half-full shuttle was just pulling in to pick up the nearly twenty laborers ready to go to work.

"Stop!" Obi-Wan shouted, waving his arms to try to keep the crowd from boarding. But the appearance of the strangely dressed Jedi had the opposite effect, and the group attempted to squeeze onto the shuttle in a panic.

Thinking quickly, Qui-Gon stepped in front of the shuttle to keep it from moving. Obi-Wan understood and dove underneath. With the simple removal of two wires, the explosive was rendered harmless. But this was just one shuttle.

Suddenly Chairman Port's voice echoed over the shuttle system's speakers.

"Evacuate the shuttles at once. Please exit and move away from the shuttles. All shuttle systems will be shut down until further notice."

Confused Vorzydiaks did as they were told. But some of them started in with their droning, and a few others rocked from side to side. Eventually most of them began to walk the long distance to work.

"We cannot allow this to be blamed on Vorzyd 5," Qui-Gon said quietly behind Obi-Wan.

Obi-Wan nodded. Just as Qui-Gon had predicted, the Freelie plan had gone horribly wrong — and so had Obi-Wan's.

"I will find out how extensive the damage is and ask the chairman to have every shuttle in the city inspected," Qui-Gon continued. "You should contact the Freelies. You must convince them to come forward before I am forced to do it for them. We haven't much time."

Obi-Wan nodded again. He had not expected

Qui-Gon to let him continue with his infiltration — not after this. He knew his Master had every right to go directly to the chairman and tell him everything. But, he realized, there was reason not to as well. It would be better for all Vorzydiaks if the Freelies came forward in peace. Forcing the kids and adults into a hostile meeting could actually make the situation worse. Qui-Gon had obviously considered this.

Obi-Wan sighed. Whatever the reason, Qui-Gon was giving Obi-Wan one last chance to do it his way. And he was grateful.

But as he watched his Master walk away, Obi-Wan was suddenly overcome by a strange feeling. He had the sense that someone was watching his every move.

Turning quickly, Obi-Wan looked up. High above him, in a window of the retiree complex, Obi-Wan thought he saw a face staring down at him. Then it disappeared.

CHAPTER 13

Obi-Wan scanned the window for another moment to see if he could catch a glimpse of the person inside. He couldn't. Still thinking about the conversation he'd just had with his Master, he walked toward the Ports' dwelling. It was time to wait for Grath.

It wasn't long before Grath appeared. When the boy had walked some distance ahead, Obi-Wan called out to him and ran to catch up. Even before he got a good look at Grath's face, Obi-Wan could tell that he was upset.

"I don't know how everything went wrong," Grath said shakily. He looked exhausted and his eyes were ringed in red. There was no sign of the charismatic, playful boy Obi-Wan had met the day before.

"There must have been a failure in the remote triggering device. It went off during . . ." Grath's voice trailed away.

"I know," Obi-Wan said, putting a hand on Grath's shoulder.

Grath swallowed. "I've called an emergency meeting. I just hope nobody notices that so many of us are not in worktraining, or at work."

Obi-Wan tried to look more optimistic than he felt. It wouldn't do any good to have Grath more worried than he already was. "Let's go," he prompted.

The meeting was held in the refuse facility. Grath managed to pull himself together, and once again looked like a leader as he stepped up on a pile of rubble to call the meeting to order.

"We have a problem," he began. "The explosives did not go off last night as planned. Instead they exploded during the morning commute."

There was a concerned murmur among the students, but an excited voice rose above the rest. It was Flip.

"And the city is in chaos!" he exclaimed. "We knew we could make a bigger bang if we just put our minds to it and waited until people were paying attention. Now our parents will really have to take notice!"

The group was silent as everyone stared at Flip.

"You did this?" Grath asked the boy. "You tampered with the remote?"

Flip nodded proudly. "Yes!" He looked up at Grath expectantly. It seemed to Obi-Wan that the younger boy was waiting for Grath to shower him with praise. But the Jedi was certain that no praise was coming.

Grath's mouth hung open for a moment before he snapped it closed. His antennae hung low over his forehead and his mouth contorted into a scowl of fury. But his eyes revealed another emotion: guilt.

Obi-Wan was not sure which of Grath's emotions was going to win out. Then Freelies all over the room began talking.

"What are we going to do now?"

"I hope my parents are okay."

"It's about time somebody took some real action."

Obi-Wan turned to see who had made this last remark. But the facility was crowded and it was impossible to tell.

Grath cleared his throat and calmed everyone down — at least for the moment.

"Many people were hurt this morning," he said gravely, "and some may not live. Our mission is to wake people up, make them see what is happening. It is not to kill them." Grath looked directly at Flip. "You should not have altered the plan," he said flatly. "It was wrong."

There was a brief moment of silence. Everyone looked at Flip. The boy looked confused, then angry. He glared up at Grath. "It was necessary," he said. "And it was the right thing to do. Now they're *really* paying attention."

The group erupted. Obi-Wan could see a split beginning to develop. Some of the kids felt that Grath was right. Acting peacefully was the only way. Others had had it with the peaceful tactics. They felt violence was a necessary part of revolution.

"The adults will never pay attention to us if we continue to act peacefully," Flip shouted. "What we've been doing so far is not working. Our pranks need to become tactics."

"We don't want to start a war!" someone shouted back. "We're talking about our parents."

"We're talking about adults who ignore us!" yelled another.

Soon everyone was shouting so loudly that Obi-Wan couldn't understand much of what was being said. He could only tell that everyone felt strongly, and that the group was divided. Then a voice rang out over the rest. It was Flip's.

"Only cowards are afraid to stand up and fight for what they need!" he shouted.

This set the Freelies off again. The camaraderie that Obi-Wan had admired in the group completely disappeared. Kids who had worked together peacefully began to shout in one another's faces. Antennae jabbed wildly in aggressive movements. The room was in chaos.

Finally Nania jumped onto a tall pile of rubble. "Stop!" she screamed. The group quieted instantly and turned to look at her. Some of the kids looked annoyed by the interruption, but nobody said anything.

"This fighting is useless," Nania said. "We need to work together or we will accomplish nothing. Let's report to our worktraining spaces before we are missed. Then tonight we can meet as planned."

Some of the Freelies grumbled aloud, but the group slowly made its way out of the facility. There was little discussion, and Obi-Wan could feel the tension in the air.

He could also feel the knot in his stomach. The division in the group was not a good sign. If the Freelies wanted to be taken seriously, they would have to come forward peacefully and talk to the adults as a cohesive group. It looked like the chances of that were getting slimmer by the minute.

Obi-Wan decided to find Grath and see what he was thinking. He circled a pile of rubble near where he had last seen him, but instead spotted Flip and a dark-haired girl he didn't recognize.

The two were clearly deep in conversation, and Obi-Wan tried to look casual as he tuned in to what they were saying.

"It's not enough," the girl said. "Grath is on their side."

He saw Flip nod slowly, and the girl leaned in closer. She spoke almost in a whisper.

"We have no choice but to take action on our own," she said. "And soon."

Obi-Wan took a step closer to the two Freelies. He wanted to hear every word. But his movement caught their attention, and they immediately split up. It was obvious they didn't want to be overheard. But he couldn't tell if they knew he'd been listening in.

Obi-Wan's mind reeled. He needed some time to clear his head. Exiting the refuse facility, he watched groups of kids make their way toward the worktraining space. He knew instinctively that worktraining was not a good place for him to think things through. So he turned in the other direction, heading toward the home-space.

Walking along, Obi-Wan now noticed the adult laborers who were still making their way to work. Some walked in pairs, talking. Others ambled along, gazing at the sky. None of them seemed desperate to get to work. And there was no audible droning. It was almost as if being forced out of their work environment gave them a new perspective.

Perhaps the adults are *ready for change,* Obi-Wan thought. He felt a small surge of hope. If he and Qui-Gon could just bring the kids and adults together, Vorzyd 4 might have a chance.

CHAPTER 14

"Vorzyd 5 must pay," Chairman Port said as he and Qui-Gon entered the Multycorp offices. "We shall contact them immediately."

Qui-Gon exhaled slowly. Although he'd expected the chairman to react in this way, he had not yet come up with a plan to stop the communication from going through.

He again questioned the wisdom of his decision to let Obi-Wan infiltrate the Freelies. He'd wanted to empower his Padawan. And he believed that Vorzyd 4 would have the best chance at a peaceful resolution if the kids came forward on their own. Unfortunately, that belief was of no help to him at the moment.

Time to think on your feet, he told himself wryly.

"I think it would be better to wait until we have the results from the shuttle inspection," Qui-Gon said rationally. Chairman Port had ordered an investigation of all the shuttles in the city, and they were waiting for the report. "The more information we have, the better."

"They are to blame!" Chairman Port railed. "They need to be punished!"

"Do we, now?" came a voice from behind them. Qui-Gon turned and saw Felana standing in the doorway. Two large Vorzydiaks flanked her on either side.

Chairman Port's face had lost all traces of anger. His expression was now a combination of confusion and fear. His large eyes were even wider than usual and his antennae twitched uncontrollably. It was obvious that he was not accustomed to unexpected political visitors — especially hostile ones.

"What are you —"

"I have come to set the record straight once and for all, Chairman," Felana said, striding into the room. She was remarkably tall for a Vorzydiak, and her upright stance made her even more so.

The chairman blinked in surprise. Qui-Gon sensed that he wanted to know how she had gotten all the way into his office without being noticed and stopped. He imagined that it probably wasn't too difficult in the chaotic aftermath of the shuttle explosions.

There were several long moments of awkward silence. Then Chairman Port straightened his jumpsuit and cleared his throat loudly. His expression shifted to one of self-righteous indignation.

"You have been sabotaging our production capabilities," he said evenly. "You resent our productivity. You wish to appear stronger to the rest of the Vorzyd system. Our computers and assembly lines are malfunctioning. It is the only explanation."

"Explanations are not my concern," Felana replied. "Your baseless accusations are. And we do not resent your productivity," she added, her eyes glinting. "On the contrary, we find your work customs to be rather tedious."

If it were not for the seriousness of the situation, Qui-Gon would have smiled at Felana's remark. The Vorzydiak kids obviously found the work customs to be tiresome as well.

"You see?" Chairman Port said, turning to Qui-Gon. "They resent us."

Qui-Gon was silent. Part of him wanted to tell Chairman Port everything. But his gut told him that this meeting was not going to bring about any kind of immediate or violent action. And he still hoped that the Freelies would come forward on their own. Besides, he had promised his Padawan that he would wait. If all went well, there would be a meeting of the minds — be-

tween those truly involved and responsible —
very soon.

"We did not resent you," Felana insisted.
"Until you began to accuse us of crimes we did
not commit." She glared at Chairman Port. "I
want all of these baseless lies to stop at once,
or we will be taking action against you in response."

Chairman Port's antennae began to twitch
again. "What kind of action?" he asked nervously.

Felana leveled her gaze at the Vorzyd 4 leader.
"A kind much worse than the sabotage you've
wrongly accused us of."

CHAPTER 15

That night, Obi-Wan met up with Grath on the shuttle platform. He looked tired, but his eyes were clear. Obi-Wan sensed that the boy had found a new sense of direction.

"Some of the adults looked content as they made their way to work today," Obi-Wan told him. "I think they enjoyed their time off."

Grath nodded. "It can work without violence," he said confidently. "People just need a little time to see how it could be."

Obi-Wan was glad to see Grath back to his old self. He didn't want to dampen his spirits by telling him about the conversation he'd over-heard between Flip and the dark-haired girl. But he couldn't keep that kind of information to himself, either.

"I overheard —"

Obi-Wan was cut short by the shuttle pulling up to the platform. Nania was driving, and she greeted Obi-Wan with a smile. Obi-Wan was grateful as he took a comfortable seat. A ride inside Nania's shuttle could be a nail-biter, but it was better than clinging to the outside of the craft.

When they arrived at the usual office building meeting place, Obi-Wan spotted Flip right away. He was standing in a corner next to the same dark-haired girl, scowling.

Grath walked right up to them. "Hi, Flip," he said in a friendly voice.

Flip didn't say anything, and his scowl deepened. It was clear that he was still angry about the reprimand he'd received earlier in the day. The girl next to him was silent as well. Watching them, Obi-Wan suddenly realized that he'd seen the girl before, away from the Freelies. She'd been visiting her grandmother at the retiree complex the first night he'd been on the planet. But she seemed totally different now — there was no trace of the warm, affectionate young girl he'd enjoyed watching and listening to.

Grath stood in front of Flip for a moment, trying to get the boy to soften. When it was clear that he wouldn't, the leader's focus shifted to the meeting at hand. He stood up on one of the desks and called everyone's attention.

"If we can show the laborers that there is

more to life than productivity without hurting them, they will help us," he said calmly.

"The laborers are too far gone," the dark-haired girl replied hotly. "Fear is the only thing that will keep them from stopping us."

Grath frowned. "That's not true, Tray," he said. "And you know it."

It didn't take long for the disagreement and anger from the earlier meeting to overtake the group. Everyone shouted to be heard. Antennae twitched and stabbed the air, punctuating shouts. Hands were balled into fists. The two groups began to separate — Grath and his followers on one side of the office and Flip and his on the other.

"We need to make ourselves known," someone yelled. "The laborers have no idea that we're pulling the pranks. They don't even think we're capable."

"We're not getting any credit," a different voice called out.

"Or blame," someone on the other side shouted.

The shouts were getting louder and louder. It was almost impossible to hear what was being said. Obi-Wan looked from one side of the room to the other, not sure what to do. He felt that some action was necessary, but he didn't want to blow his cover.

Suddenly the lights outside the office blinked on. Voices echoed outside, and footsteps thundered up the stairs.

Grath looked up, alarmed. The kids were suddenly silent.

The Freelies had been discovered.

CHAPTER 16

The footsteps and voices got louder as they came closer. The Freelies began to look worriedly at one another, their antennae twitching in fear.

Out of the corner of his eye, Obi-Wan saw Flip toss a small capsule to the ground. A thick, green smoke immediately began to billow into the room. Interestingly, the smoke did not seem to irritate the Freelies' lungs. There was no coughing or sputtering among the group.

"This way," Flip said calmly. He led the kids out of the office through a secret exit, down a tunnel, and up several flights of stairs. When they emerged through a heavy durasteel doorway, they were standing on the roof of a neighboring workspace building. It was dark, but the stars in the sky gave off a dim light.

All was quiet below. The kids were safe.

No sooner were the Freelies on the roof than

Flip turned toward Obi-Wan. "There's something you don't know!" he shouted to the group. "Grath has been keeping it from you. This boy has been sent here to stop us. He is a Jedi — and a traitor!"

There was an audible gasp as the Freelies gaped at Obi-Wan. For a moment Obi-Wan sensed that the group wasn't sure this was the truth — and thought he might be safe.

The moment passed quickly.

"It's true!" the dark-haired girl shouted. "I've seen him at the retirement complex. My grandmother is there, and he was spying on us!"

"Yes, Tray, he is a Jedi." Grath lowered his head in defeat.

Obi-Wan closed his eyes for a moment. He'd had no idea that Grath knew he was a Jedi. Taking a deep breath, he tried to gather strength. He was not looking forward to what was coming. Someone pulled at his hood, exposing his antennae-less head.

"Traitor!" someone shouted.

"Grath is a liar, not a leader!" Flip yelled.

"What kind of leader doesn't trust his team enough to tell them the simple truth?" came a quieter voice.

Kids on both sides of the violence issue were coming out against Grath and Obi-Wan. Only a few stood by Grath.

"Grath has to make difficult decisions for all of us," Nania said reasonably. "We may not like each and every one, but he makes them for the good of the group. He has never led us astray."

"The Jedi should still leave us," Tray spoke out. "Immediately."

There was silence as the group nodded — almost unanimously. Only Grath's head remained still.

Obi-Wan looked to Grath for support, hoping he would say something to the group. Grath looked distraught, but he kept quiet.

Obi-Wan felt defeated, but knew he could not just walk away.

"Peace is the only way to true victory," he told the Freelies. "If you continue down this path you'll build a permanent wall between yourselves and the workers. There will be no chance for dialogue, or a new way of life."

Obi-Wan looked beseechingly at the group, his eyes moving from one face to another. None of their expressions had changed. There was no way for him to convince them.

Obi-Wan dropped his head and turned toward the stairs. The last thing he saw before the door slid closed behind him was the smiles on Tray's and Flip's faces.

Obi-Wan's mind was spinning as he left the rooftop. He felt like a fool. Why didn't he suspect that Grath knew he was a Jedi all along? The infiltration had been too easy, he now realized. Obi-Wan felt ashamed for not figuring it out earlier. He had wanted his plan to work so badly that he assumed everything was going just fine. Only it wasn't.

Obi-Wan made his way through the streets to the homespace. In the back of his mind was a voice that reminded him that he hadn't been entirely honest with the Freelies, either. He hadn't told them he was a Jedi.

But I was acting for the good of the planet, he told himself. *I was trying to bring everyone to a peaceful solution.*

This all felt much like the situation on Melida/Daan, Obi-Wan realized. When Obi-Wan had joined the Young, he was certain that he was doing the right thing. But in the end he was not sure that the Young were on the right path. And it had not taken him long to know that leaving the Jedi order was not the right path for him.

At first glance, the situation here on Vorzyd 4 seemed totally different from the one on Melida/Daan. Harmless, really. But now Obi-Wan could not see many differences. And the similarities were screaming in his ears.

The arguing Freelies. The explosions. The inability of the generations to talk openly together.

Worst of all, Obi-Wan knew, he was no longer

in a position to help. The kids didn't trust him. And why should the adults believe someone who had been keeping secrets from them all along?

Not sure what else to do, Obi-Wan headed back to his room at the retirement complex. He had not been there long when Qui-Gon arrived.

Obi-Wan knew his Master was concerned about him — and probably the situation as well. With a sigh, he began to tell him all that had happened.

"Someone must have tipped off the adults," Obi-Wan began.

Qui-Gon nodded. "I did not say anything, as I promised I would not," he said. "But I did over-hear the building maintenance team reporting a disturbance to Chairman Port. They were acting on a tip."

Obi-Wan had not suspected that Qui-Gon was responsible for the intrusion, but was glad to hear his Master confirm that he was not.

"A group of adults stormed the secret meet-ing," Obi-Wan said. "But one of the kids, Flip, dropped a smoke capsule and led everyone to safety."

"He was well prepared for just such an inva-sion," Qui-Gon said pointedly.

Obi-Wan nodded. "I thought that at the time," he said. "Perhaps *he* was the informer. It seemed too simple. But much more has happened since then. . . ."

Obi-Wan trailed off. It was getting difficult to look his Master in the eye. He felt responsible for the state of the situation between the kids and adults. Once again he had the feeling that his instincts had been all wrong.

"Go on," Qui-Gon said gently. His eyes were full of empathy. But somehow that didn't make Obi-Wan feel any better. In fact, it made him feel worse. He didn't deserve understanding right now. Things on Vorzyd 4 were worse than when they'd arrived.

And it was all his fault.

CHAPTER 17

Qui-Gon could see that his Padawan was struggling. He was tempted to push him further to see if he would open up, but knew that was not the right choice. What Obi-Wan needed was a bit of time, just as Qui-Gon himself did on occasion.

The room in the retirement complex was quiet for several minutes. Then Qui-Gon spoke.

"I think we should go outside and spar," he said. "It has been too long since we did lightsaber training together."

Qui-Gon was hoping that the physical activity would help his Padawan release some tension — and piece things together in his mind. Regardless, focusing on something entirely different would be a good change of pace.

Obi-Wan seemed reluctant as they exited the building. But once he was outside and facing his Master, his eyes flashed with an intensity that surprised Qui-Gon. The young Jedi ignited his lightsaber, and Qui-Gon did the same.

The two Jedi circled each other slowly with their lightsabers raised, as if in a dance. Obi-Wan moved gracefully, his eyes locked on Qui-Gon's. It was as if he were challenging him to do something, to make the first move.

Qui-Gon did. He brought his lightsaber down in a powerful strike — once, twice, three times. Obi-Wan was there to block each blow. The graceful arcs he made with his blade were confident and accurate. His eyes never left his Master's face.

Qui-Gon suddenly realized that his Padawan's lightsaber skills had improved significantly in the past months. His physical energy was exceptional — young and true. Obi-Wan was fighting like a Jedi Knight.

Not to mention trusting his instincts, Qui-Gon thought wryly. He suddenly had the feeling that one day the boy would beat him. And that such a day might not be so far away.

The two Jedi dodged and weaved with incredible speed, their ignited blue and green blades blurs of energy in the Vorzyd night. But behind them pulsed something even stronger — Jedi will. Obi-Wan wanted to be treated as an equal, Qui-Gon knew. But while he had grown up a lot in the last four years, he was only seventeen. He still had much to learn.

With each stroke, Qui-Gon pushed Obi-Wan farther back. It was not terribly difficult. But even as he advanced on his Padawan, Qui-Gon had the feeling that Obi-Wan was allowing him to do it — that the Padawan was somehow in control.

He was. In a flash of blinding green light Obi-Wan swung, ducked, and turned. His blue eyes flashed and a small smile turned up the corners of his lips. He now had the upper hand.

Qui-Gon was accustomed to this kind of haughty strategy coming from an enemy. But it was slightly unnerving to see it in his own Padawan learner. And yet it had worked.

As if picking up on his Master's thoughts, Obi-Wan stepped up the pace an additional notch. Now he was swinging repeatedly and with phenomenal strength, pushing Qui-Gon in a wide arc around the courtyard. His green blade was a bright blur in the darkness, and his entire body moved with certainty and empowerment.

Qui-Gon had to concentrate — hard — to keep ahead of his Padawan. They had fought side by side often enough for him to be able to guess what Obi-Wan would do next. Of course, the same was true of Obi-Wan. And once in a while the young Jedi blocked a blow so quickly that Qui-Gon knew the boy had known exactly what was coming.

With a flash and a buzz, the lightsabers met in a raised cross. Both men were breathless, sweating from the exertion. This had been no lighthearted spar.

Obi-Wan looked up at his Master, his eyes bright and intense. It was clear that he had not actually won the match, but that he had stated his case firmly. Something had changed between them. Obi-Wan had taken yet another step toward becoming a Jedi Knight, and Qui-Gon was closer than ever to letting him go.

Without speaking, the two Jedi switched off their lightsabers and headed back into the retirement complex.

"You must go to Grath," Qui-Gon said quietly. "The students and the laborers have much to teach one another."

Obi-Wan nodded. "I agree," he said. "As you have had much to teach me. I am grateful, Master."

Qui-Gon felt a surge of pride. Obi-Wan was a good man, and would be a great Jedi Knight. "We learn from each other, Padawan," he said. "But thank you."

Obi-Wan nodded. "I think I should find Grath immediately," he said. "I see now that there is still a chance for us to stop the dispute, to get the two sides to listen to each other. But we do not have much time. I think that deep down, the students and the adults want the same thing."

"Yes, deep down," Qui-Gon agreed.

CHAPTER 18

Obi-Wan slept soundly through the night and awoke with a clear head. He knew exactly what needed to be done, and was prepared to do it.

After donning his Jedi robes, he left the retirement complex, walked over to the Ports' homespace, and knocked on the door. It seemed as though Grath were standing right on the other side, because the door slid open immediately. Obi-Wan was surprised to see Nania behind him.

"We were just getting ready to come look for you," Grath explained. He looked a bit sheepish. "I'm glad you've come."

Grath stepped aside and Obi-Wan entered the dwelling. Nania led them all to the table.

"I'm so sorry, Obi-Wan," Grath said as soon as they were sitting down. "I knew you were a Jedi because I overheard my father. I should have told you. But I thought you might not want to help if you knew I knew. Or that your Master would not let you. And I didn't think that all of the Freelies would accept help from a Jedi."

Grath spoke quickly and clearly, and his words felt genuine. Obi-Wan could see why he was the leader of the Freelies.

"I deceived you as well," Obi-Wan admitted. "I knew that it was dishonest not to tell you that I was a Jedi. But I felt it was the best way to learn what was happening on your planet, and how to help."

Grath's eyes lit up. "I know," he said. "And I think you *can* help. We need to get through to our parents. They are not our enemy. You have seen firsthand what our relationships are like. They are crumbling. We need to rebuild the foundations. You might have the power to help facilitate that."

"Both sides could be a problem at this point," Nania added. "The adults suspect that we have been pulling the pranks, so they may be hostile. Especially because they've been accusing Vorzyd 5. We've caused a lot of trouble. And now the Freelies are divided."

"I did not tip off the adults," Obi-Wan said earnestly. He wanted Grath and Nania to know he would not betray them in such a way.

"We know that," Grath said.

"It was Flip," Nania added. "I overheard him

and Tray laughing about how easy it was to fool the rest of the group." She reached over and put a hand on Obi-Wan's arm. "We know you've only been trying to help us, Obi-Wan," she said. "That's your job as a Jedi, isn't it?"

"Yes, I suppose it is," Obi-Wan said.

"But things keep getting worse and worse," Grath said, suddenly looking a bit defeated. "We used to do this just for fun," he said. "You know, for something to do."

"It went on like that for a while, and it was okay," Nania said. "We were having fun. We worked hard together doing the planning and carrying out the pranks. And nobody got hurt."

"But then we changed the rules," Grath continued. "We wanted to wake up the laborers — our parents and grandparents. Then my father began to accuse Vorzyd 5." His voice suddenly held a tinge of bitterness. "We started to interfere with productivity, because that was all they seemed to care about. We just wanted to be noticed. . . ."

Grath's voice trailed off and his eyes fell to the floor. "We're not so sure about the pranks anymore," he admitted. "We never intended for those explosives to go off when laborers were in the shuttles. We never meant for anyone to get hurt."

"Now we want to stop what we have in the

works," Nania continued. "But we're not sure we can convince Flip and the Freelies on his side to call it off — that violence isn't the way."

Obi-Wan raised an eyebrow. "This next prank would be violent?" he asked.

"It's not actually supposed to be," Grath replied. "But it was going to be explosive. And with the way things have been going . . ."

His voice trailed off once more. But this time he looked up at the ceiling. "I don't know what's happened to Flip," he said mournfully. "He used to be such a great person. A real friend. I always thought he looked up to me."

"He did," Nania said. "But Flip is his own person. You can't blame yourself for his thoughts and actions."

Obi-Wan's heart went out to Grath. He knew what it was like to feel responsible — he had felt that way so many times. When his friends were in danger. When his rivals had died.

"I'll bet he still looks up to you," Obi-Wan said, remembering how hurt Flip had seemed when Grath came down on him for setting off the explosive devices during the morning commute. "I think his anger might be a mask for his hurt. He wants you to be proud of him."

"I am proud of him," Grath said. "In a way. I just think his energy is misdirected."

"It's important for you to move forward and

make the right decisions. For everybody—including Flip," Obi-Wan counseled. "It's time to meet with the adults, to tell them what is going on. You need to confide in them."

Grath let out his breath slowly. "I know," he said. "But I don't know where to begin."

"I can set up the meeting for you," Obi-Wan said. "And Qui-Gon will help counsel the laborers."

Grath sighed. "Okay," he said. "But I have a feeling that talking to the laborers might be easier than convincing the Freelies to call off the latest prank — and to show up at the meeting."

CHAPTER 19

That evening, over a Vorzyd supper of taste-less broth and a tough flatbread, Obi-Wan told his Master of his meeting with Grath and Nania.

"I really think we can turn the situation into a positive one," he said confidently. "The Freelies have to see that meeting with the laborers is the right thing to do. It's the best thing for everybody."

"I agree, Padawan," Qui-Gon said. "And I think I should accompany you to this Freelie meeting. There is much at stake."

Obi-Wan could not help but feel chided. Didn't his Master think he could handle the situation? Wasn't it clear that he was approaching the problem in a new way?

Obi-Wan swallowed his utensilful of broth and looked across the table at his Master. "I would like to go alone," he said slowly. "To finish what I have started by myself. We will both be at the meeting between the Freelies and the laborers, of course." Obi-Wan hoped this last comment might sway his Master a bit.

There was a moment of silence before Qui-Gon spoke. "Very well," he said. "I understand that it could be important for you to go alone. My presence might upset the balance you have been trying to create. I will contact Chairman Port and make sure the laborers are ready to meet. I will need to be present when he contacts Vorzyd 5 to apologize. And I may know a few others who would be interested in coming to the Freelie/laborer meeting as well," he added thoughtfully.

Obi-Wan wondered who his Master was talking about, but a knock on their retiree room door halted their conversation. A second later the metal portal slid open and Grath stood in the doorway. He looked sheepishly at Qui-Gon, as if he wasn't sure how to greet a Jedi Master.

Qui-Gon got to his feet and lowered his head slightly before Grath.

"It's an honor to meet the leader of the Freelies," Qui-Gon said.

Grath looked surprised, but Obi-Wan just smiled. His Master was exceptionally skilled at setting others at ease.

"Obi-Wan has told me much about you," Qui-Gon continued with a friendly smile.

Grath smiled back. "It's an honor to meet you as well," he said. "And I'd like to thank you for your help. I'm hoping Vorzyd 4 will be on a new path before you leave."

"That is my wish as well," Qui-Gon agreed as he began to clear the eating utensils from the table. Obi-Wan sensed that it was his way of not intruding on their departure. Silently grateful, Obi-Wan left the room with Grath.

The two crossed the courtyard and waited for Nania to pick them up in the shuttle. In spite of his apparent confidence back in the retirement complex, Obi-Wan felt quite nervous. What if the Freelies wouldn't listen to what he and Grath had to say? What if they still thought he was a traitor?

By the time they got to the refuse facility, Obi-Wan was practicing a calming breathing technique. But he did not have to worry. The Freelies were quiet as they heard Grath out.

"I must apologize to you all for not telling you that we had a Jedi among us," Grath said from atop a heap of rubble. "But at the time I thought I was doing the right thing."

While he listened to Grath, Obi-Wan looked around the facility. Kids were listening intently, and many were nodding. Only Tray stood apart, alone in a corner, looking angry. There was no sign of Flip.

"Obi-Wan has come to help us," Grath went on. "He understands what we are trying to do. And he can bring us and the laborers together."

"No!" Tray shouted, stamping her foot. Looking at her, Obi-Wan wondered why she was so bent on violence. What did she want to accomplish?

There was a murmur in the crowd, and kids began to speak. But they were much more orderly than they had been the previous day, taking turns and listening to what others were saying. Obi-Wan took this as a good sign.

"They don't care about us," someone said. "It's all about productivity."

"And they won't listen," another Freelie added. "They'll just stop the pranks, and the pranks are . . ." The boy struggled to find the right words.

"I agree," Grath interrupted. "Our coming together to make the pranks happen is the only fun I've had, and could be the best thing I've ever done. But we are not solving the problem. We are not getting any closer to our parents. We have to start somewhere if we are going to bring about the changes we need."

There was a moment of silence as the Freelies looked at one another. Obi-Wan noticed that Tray's antennae were jabbing at the air, as if fighting something invisible. But the others seemed to be getting what Grath was saying. They understood that violence wasn't the answer.

"You do not have to come to the meeting if you are opposed," Nania said, looking directly at Tray. "But we hope you will. It is for all of us. It is the only way."

Nania kept her eyes locked on Tray, as if she expected an argument. But the girl remained sullen and silent. Then Nania's antennae straightened.

"Where is Flip?" she asked.

Tray shrugged. "I do not know," she said. But there was a glint in her eyes that made Obi-Wan suspect she wasn't telling the truth.

Obi-Wan switched on his comlink. It was time to contact Qui-Gon. The device crackled for a moment, and then he heard his Master's voice.

"The Freelies have agreed to meet," Obi-Wan said.

"That is good news," Qui-Gon replied. "We are in the Multycorp annex next to Chairman Port's office. We have made peace with Vorzyd 5, and a large group of laborers has gathered here, along with some retirees. We are anxious to get started."

"Excellent," Obi-Wan said. For the first time in days he felt relieved, and truly hopeful. "We are on our way."

Obi-Wan ended the communication and climbed onto a small pile of rubble. "The laborers are waiting to meet with us — to hear what we have to say," he told the Freelies. "Some of the retirees are there as well. They want to begin the dialogue. We should all head over to the Multycorp annex at once."

There was audible excitement as the Freelies began to chatter among themselves. Antennae all over the room were bouncing up and down. Obi-Wan turned to look for Tray, and saw her sink to the ground. A look of horror was frozen on her face.

"But my grandmother —" she stammered. "No." She looked up at Grath and Obi-Wan. "The Multycorp annex is going to explode."

CHAPTER 20

The Freelies grew completely silent as Tray's words sank in.

"What?" Grath said. "What did you say?"

Tray's eyes were full of tears. "The Multycorp annex is going to explode," she repeated. "We thought it would be empty. There were no meetings on the roster."

Obi-Wan reached for his comlink. If he could tell Qui-Gon what was happening, they might be able to stop the explosion. But before he could even attempt to make a transmission Tray was shaking her head.

Obi-Wan tried the comlink, but there was only interference and static.

"It won't work anymore," she said woodenly. "We've scrambled communication." She pointed to her timepiece. "We're too late."

Tray leaped to her feet. "We have to stop the explosion!" she shouted. "Come on!"

Leading the way, Tray rushed out to the maintenance shuttle and climbed into the cockpit seat. For a moment, Nania looked as though she might try to take the controls from her, but she changed her mind. Tray needed something to do.

Unfortunately, Tray was not much of a pilot. If a ride with Nania was an adventure, a ride with Tray was a hazard. The shuttle lurched and bounced, tossing the other Freelies around in the back.

As he slammed into his seat, Obi-Wan tried to clear his mind. He wanted to send Qui-Gon a warning about the explosion. But there was so much anxiety and commotion in the shuttle it was difficult to concentrate. He closed his eyes and shut out all of the noise and emotion. Gathering the Force around him, he sent a warning to Qui-Gon. *Get everyone out of the Multycorp annex,* he told him. *Now.*

Obi-Wan opened his eyes to find Grath staring at him. "I hope whatever you just did works," the boy said in a shaky voice. "If anything happens to my father because of me, because of what I've done. . . ." he trailed off, suddenly at a loss for words.

Obi-Wan tried to reassure Grath. "We're doing all we can. We mustn't lose hope," he said.

But Obi-Wan himself had a foreboding feeling. They might be too late.

"It's all my fault," Grath went on. "I started to change the pranks. I wanted to get their attention. To make them see . . ." Grath's eyes filled with tears as he stared out of the shuttle portal. "And now my father, the leader of the planet, is in danger."

"It's not your fault, Grath," Tray piped up, her voice wavering. "It's mine." She made a sharp turn and the shuttle banked to the left. There was a groan from a few Freelies who were thrown against the shuttle wall.

"I convinced Flip that the pranks should become violent. I told him you would respect him for taking the next step, that you would be proud. . . ." Tray took a hand off the controls to wipe her eyes, sending the shuttle into a nosedive. It skidded against the ground before Tray righted it again.

"And he believed me," she said with a sob. "He believed every word I said."

Finally the shuttle rounded a corner and the Multycorp annex came into view. Obi-Wan let out a huge sigh of relief. It was still standing.

But before the shuttle got close enough for anyone to shout a warning, a huge explosion rocked the workspace. Chunks of metal, cement, and other debris shot into the air as the front of the Multycorp annex exploded, collapsing in on itself.

"No!" Grath screamed, covering his face with his hands. Nania stared ahead, too shocked to speak. Tray slumped over the shuttle's controls. Obi-Wan scanned the area through the viewscreen, waiting for the dust to clear. Did Qui-Gon get his message? Did the Vorzydiaks get out in time? Obi-Wan sensed that his Master was nearby, but could not tell if he was all right.

Obi-Wan immediately saw a group of people. Some were crouched, others lay on the ground amid the rubble. There was not much movement.

Forcing open the shuttle door, Obi-Wan raced toward them. He desperately hoped that he was not running toward a scene of death.

CHAPTER 21

The explosion site was in chaos. Vorzydiak laborers and retirees were everywhere, lying on the ground, droning, and nursing injuries. All of them were in shock. Obi-Wan followed Grath and Tray as the Vorzydiaks searched the crowd for their families.

At last Obi-Wan spotted Qui-Gon's brown robe. His Master was kneeling beside a body on the ground. Next to him was Chairman Port.

"Father!" Grath shouted and sprinted ahead.

Chairman Port turned. His face was singed. With one hand he protected the injured arm that hung awkwardly at his side. Being careful not to hurt his broken arm, Grath stepped close to his father. They did not speak but instead embraced using their antennae, letting their feelers entwine, assuring each other that they were going to be all right.

Obi-Wan hurried toward Qui-Gon. He was relieved to see his Master was not injured, but the Jedi did not embrace. The look on Qui-Gon's face stopped Obi-Wan in his tracks. Tray's grandmother was the figure on the ground. Her eyes were closed and there was blood on her face.

Tray dropped to her knees beside her grandmother, unable to speak.

"She's going to be fine," Qui-Gon said softly. "She was hit on the head by a small piece of falling debris on her way out of the building."

The old woman's eyes fluttered open and she reached out for her granddaughter. Tray took her hand, but her face remained a mask of horror. Obi-Wan knew she was blaming herself.

Qui-Gon put his hand on Tray's shoulder. "Your grandmother is a brave woman."

Tray looked gratefully at Qui-Gon through tear-filled eyes. He returned her gaze reassuringly before turning to Obi-Wan.

"Thanks to your warning almost everyone was able to get out of the building in time."

"Almost everyone?" Obi-Wan asked. Qui-Gon did not need to say anything else. Obi-Wan knew who had been left inside. "Flip," he said quietly, not wanting to upset Tray further. But she overheard.

"No!" Tray sobbed. "No, not Flip. We've got to find him. We've got to get him out."

Obi-Wan nodded solemnly. Of course they

needed to find Flip. He only hoped they would find him alive.

Grath shouted and waved the growing group of Freelies to the corner of what had been the front of the Multycorp annex.

"There's a sound coming from the basement," he explained. "We have to get in there."

The team of laborers had searched the rubble for only a few minutes before they first heard the soft pinging. It could have been a piece of machinery still trying to operate. It could have been a wild creature. Or it could have been Flip.

A dozen large laborers gathered together and pushed with all of their strength on a heavy beam that blocked access to the basement level. It didn't move.

"Lift together," Grath shouted. "On three."

Several of the laborers looked skeptically at the young Freelies. But they made room for them around the beam.

"One, two, three," Grath counted. Working together, the group lifted the beam, easily sliding it over until they'd created an opening about a meter wide.

"Brace the side," Grath shouted.

The opening wasn't much, but it was big enough for Obi-Wan to squeeze through.

"Hurry, Obi-Wan," Grath urged as the young

Jedi began to lower himself into the darkened basement. He didn't need to ask twice. Obi-Wan knew that the remains of the Multycorp annex were unstable at best. Even with the beam braced over the entrance, the chance of a collapse was great. And if Flip was still alive his time could be limited.

Obi-Wan paused a moment, letting his eyes adjust to the darkness. He listened for the pinging. It seemed to be coming from a spot ahead of him and to the left. It was getting less frequent.

Suddenly dirt and pebbles poured down onto Obi-Wan's head.

"Look out," called a voice above him. "I'm coming with you."

The light from the opening was blocked for a moment. Then Tray dropped down beside Obi-Wan.

"The noise is coming from over there," Obi-Wan pointed. He started to lead the way but Tray rushed past him.

"Flip?" she yelled. "Flip? Hang on, we're coming." The Vorzydiak girl ducked around a large piece of machinery. She moved quickly and easily in the cramped quarters and disappeared from view. But Obi-Wan could still hear her calling to her friend.

"Flip? Flip!" Tray's exclamation left no doubt

that she had found the boy. Obi-Wan pushed past a pile of rubble to join them.

"Flip," Tray repeated more quietly. Together Obi-Wan and Tray heaved the piece of durasteel bracing that pinned Flip to the floor off his chest. Dropping down beside him, Tray took the boy's hand. She loosened his grip on the scrap of durasteel he'd been pounding on the brace as a distress signal.

Except for a large bruise on his forehead, Flip appeared to be okay. But even though the brace was no longer holding him down, he couldn't get up. Watching him struggle to get enough air to speak, Obi-Wan realized that he was in bad shape. Flip coughed and winced in pain.

"Lie down," Obi-Wan instructed. "Don't try to move or speak. Then he turned to Tray. "Stay with him while I get the medics."

As Obi-Wan made his way back to the basement opening he heard Tray speaking softly.

"I'm so sorry," she whispered. A sob caught in her throat. "I was wrong."

CHAPTER 22

Tray stood as close as she could to the gravstretcher as Flip was slowly maneuvered out of the basement. Grath fidgeted nervously as they emerged. It was obvious to Qui-Gon that the boy wanted to talk to Flip, but that something was holding him back.

Qui-Gon glanced at his Padawan, mentally urging him to coax Grath forward. But Obi-Wan was already approaching the Freelie leader. Qui-Gon could not hear what Obi-Wan spoke into Grath's ear, but whatever it was gave him the courage to take a few steps toward the wounded boy.

Grath put his hand over Flip's and bent close to his face, speaking quietly. Although Flip could not respond, the look in his eyes said that all was forgiven. Grath and the younger boy touched their antennae together briefly. Then

Flip's antennae drooped across his face, and his body went still. Flip was gone.

"No!" Tray sobbed. She leaned over Flip's body, laying her head on his chest. "No," she whispered. "Not you."

Grath put a comforting hand on Tray's back. "It's not your fault, Tray," he said softly. "Flip was his own person, and made his own choices. We were all doing what we thought needed to be done."

Tray looked up at Grath gratefully, her large eyes full of tears. Then she dropped her head. "But our way was not the right one," she said.

"I do not think so, either," Grath said. "But now we are on another path. The path to peace."

Tray nodded slowly. Qui-Gon sensed that over time she would come to terms with Flip's death. But it would not happen quickly.

Grath gazed down at Flip's lifeless body, then leaned over and briefly said good-bye. Tray did the same, then several other Freelies. The medics covered Flip with a heavy gray cloth and loaded the gravstretcher into the transport.

Grath, Tray, and Obi-Wan stood silently together as the transport took off. Slowly more Freelies gathered around the trio, twining their arms and droning. The sound was soft at first, then grew louder and more intense. It was full of pain and sorrow. The young group had been through a lot, and would now need to cope with a death among them. It would not be easy, Qui-Gon knew. And there was still much work and challenge to come.

When the last of the injured Vorzydiaks had been taken to med units and the dust had finally settled, there was a moment of calm. But soon the moment of peace was over.

A large Vorzydiak laborer pointed an angry finger at the Freelies. "Look at what you've done," he said, gesturing toward the rubble. "How can we work?"

"Have you no respect?" asked another angry laborer, shouting at the Freelies. "Have we taught you nothing?"

"You've taught us plenty," answered a voice from the cluster of Freelies. "You've taught us that work is all you care about. And that *this* is what we have to do to get your attention."

Very quickly the scene erupted into a giant shouting match between the Freelies and the laborers. Qui-Gon watched from the sidelines beside a handful of retirees. The argument was going nowhere, each side convinced that the other was at fault. Qui-Gon was about to take a step forward when Obi-Wan separated himself from the Freelies and moved to stand between the two groups.

"It is useless to lay blame," he said in a commanding voice. "I think you can all agree that the damage has been done." Obi-Wan spoke slowly and calmly, looking into the faces of laborers and Freelies alike. Qui-Gon felt a wave of pride well up within him. When had Obi-Wan become so wise?

"You must work together to heal the wounds that have shown themselves today." Obi-Wan directed his plea toward the laborers. But in spite of the truth in Obi-Wan's words, Qui-Gon could tell the adult Vorzydiaks were not convinced.

"My Padawan is right," Qui-Gon said as he joined Obi-Wan in the space between the factions. "The generations have much to offer one another." He placed an arm around Obi-Wan's shoulder. "In time you may understand that there is more to life than work and productivity. You do not have to agree all of the time, but if you take time to listen, to learn from one another, the work you do together will become infinitely more rewarding."

The words resonated within Qui-Gon as he spoke them. He hoped Obi-Wan understood that he was not just speaking about the Vorzydiaks. He was talking about the two of them. How much they taught each other. How happy it made them to work together, to depend on each other, to know that they would always be there for each other, even when they did not agree.

With a glance at his apprentice he saw that Obi-Wan understood. The two Jedi did not need antennae to communicate emotions. Their bond was strong.

Qui-Gon's words reached some of the Vorzydiaks, too. But many remained unconvinced.

"Who are you to tell us what to do?" one of the laborers asked Qui-Gon and Obi-Wan angrily.

Chairman Port struggled to the front of the crowd and Grath rushed to help him. "You are right," Port said to the angry Vorzydiak. "The Jedi are not the ones who should solve our problems. Together we have created this disaster." He leaned heavily on his son. "And together we must work to resolve it."

CHAPTER 23

In only two days the retirement complex had changed significantly. Almost every door stood open, including the front entrance that led to the courtyard. After work hours, Vorzydiaks of all ages drifted in and out. Occasionally the sound of laughter even made its way down the once-deserted halls.

Obi-Wan walked with Qui-Gon toward the exit, marveling at the change. The Vorzydiaks would need time to mourn Flip's death and the damage he had done. The rift between the generations would not heal quickly. But Obi-Wan was hopeful.

The irregular bleat of a Vorzydiak echoed down the hall. It made Obi-Wan smile, and then stop in his tracks. It sounded like Grath.

"Master, wait," Obi-Wan called. He rushed back down the hall toward the familiar noise, and was not disappointed.

Grath sat in a circle of chairs in one of the complex bedrooms. Taking a second look, Obi-Wan noticed that instead of sleeping couches this room had been filled with chairs and tables positioned for conversation. It had been converted into a sort of leisure lounge.

Obi-Wan was pleased to see the converted room, but immediately sensed a sadness in the air.

Grath stood and greeted his friend. "We were just talking about Flip," he explained. "The things he did are still very painful, but sharing memories is helping all of us." He gestured to the others in the room — a few Freelies, his father, Tray, and Tray's grandmother, Ina. They all waved their antennae at Obi-Wan in greeting.

Grath turned back to Obi-Wan. "You are not leaving yet, are you?"

Obi-Wan was glad when Qui-Gon came into the room behind him and interrupted Grath's question. They were, in fact, on their way back to Coruscant.

"Chairman Port." Qui-Gon's voice was warm and deep. He crossed the small room in two steps and held out his hand to the chairman. "You're away from your office. Don't you have work to do?" Qui-Gon's eyes were alight with amusement.

Chairman Port took Qui-Gon's hand but did

not return his smile. "You have shown us there is more important work to do," he said humbly. "We are grateful."

"We were on our way to thank you," Grath said. "But we stopped to talk to Ina and were sharing some memories of Flip."

Obi-Wan smiled slightly. The generations of Vorzydiaks were finally spending time together, sharing emotions. And in spite of the pain caused by Flip's death, they seemed to be enjoying it.

"We wish to thank you," Chairman Port said formally, "for assisting us in our relations with Vorzyd 5, and . . ." Chairman Port struggled to find the words. His flailing antennae touched the top of his son's head, tousling his hair. "And in our relationships here on Vorzyd 4."

Qui-Gon nodded, accepting the thanks.

"Oh, and we have a new plan," Tray said excitedly.

For a brief moment, Obi-Wan thought she was talking about another Freelie prank.

"The young people are helping to make an outdoor space for us," Ina explained.

"The laborers will also be helping," Grath added. "Father is shortening the work week by one day so that there will be time."

The Vorzydiaks looked from one to the other. Their antennae waved gently back and forth as if they were riding a gentle breeze. Obi-Wan didn't think he had seen any of them looking as alive and happy as they did right now.

"There is still much to be done," Chairman Port said. "But we have begun. And together we shall finish."

"I believe that you will," Qui-Gon agreed. "But I'm afraid it is time for us to get back to Coruscant. We have our own work to do."

"Of course, of course," Chairman Port agreed.

The Vorzydiaks bid good-bye to the Jedi, and Obi-Wan followed his Master down the hall. They did have work to do, Obi-Wan knew. And it was work they needed to do together.

"Our work is well begun, my Padawan," Qui-Gon said, breaking into Obi-Wan's thoughts. They stepped outside into the courtyard, and Qui-Gon stopped and turned to his apprentice. "And though we are beyond the beginning of our journey, we are not quite at the end."

Obi-Wan nodded. "I know. I still have much to learn."

"Yet you have already grown so much," Qui-Gon acknowledged. "I am proud of you, Obi-Wan. Proud of what you have become. It is an honor to teach you, to work with you. I could not ask for a better Padawan learner."

Obi-Wan beamed. "To work then," he said.

"Yes," Qui-Gon agreed. "To work."

The stunning series finale!

STAR WARS

JEDI APPRENTICE

Special Edition #2: The Followers

The followers of a society devoted to the dark side rise to challenge two generations of Jedi—Qui-Gon Jinn and Obi-Wan Kenobi, and then an older Obi-Wan and his apprentice, Anakin Skywalker.

An adventure set between Episode I and Episode II.

Coming next month!
Wherever books are sold.

LUCAS BOOKS

SCHOLASTIC

SW0202